FRESHMAN YEAR

CHARCOAL
♥MOM
CAMPUS MAP

FRESHMAN YEAR

SARAH MAI

Christy Ottaviano Books

Little, Brown and Company
New York Boston

ABOUT THIS BOOK

This book was edited by Jessica Anderson and designed by Ann Dwyer.
The production was supervised by Bernadette Flinn, and the production editor was Jake Regier.
The text was set in Action Man, and the display type is Caroni.

Lettering by Mercedes Campos López

Christy Ottaviano Books
Hachette Book Group
1290 Avenue of the Americas, New York, NY 10104
Visit us at LBYR.com

First Edition: February 2024

Christy Ottaviano Books is an imprint of Little, Brown and Company.
The Christy Ottaviano Books name and logo are trademarks of Hachette Book Group, Inc.

Little, Brown and Company books may be purchased in bulk for business, educational, or promotional use. For information, please contact your local bookseller or the Hachette Book Group Special Markets Department at special.markets@hbgusa.com.

Library of Congress Cataloging-in-Publication Data
Names: Mai, Sarah, author, illustrator.
Title: Freshman year / Sarah Mai.
Description: First edition. | New York ; Boston : Little, Brown and Company, 2024. | "Christy Ottaviano Books." | Audience: Ages 14–18. | Summary: Chronicles the constant angst, hilarity, and self-doubt enmeshed in the experience of going away to college—all through the eyes of an eighteen-year-old burgeoning comics artist.
Identifiers: LCCN 2022004092 | ISBN 9780316401074 (hardcover) | ISBN 9780316401173 (trade paperback) | ISBN 9780316401272 (ebook)
Subjects: CYAC: Graphic novels. | Universities and colleges—Fiction. | Stress (Psychology)—Fiction. | Friendship—Fiction. | LCGFT: Graphic novels.
Classification: LCC PZ7.7.M33257 Fr 2024 | DDC 741.5/973—dc23/eng/20220428
LC record available at https://lccn.loc.gov/2022004092

ISBNs: 978-0-316-40107-4 (hardcover), 978-0-316-40117-3 (pbk.), 978-0-316-40127-2 (ebook), 978-0-316-56850-0 (ebook), 978-0-316-56851-7 (ebook)

PRINTED IN CHINA

1010

Hardcover: 10 9 8 7 6 5 4 3 2 1
Paperback: 10 9 8 7 6 5 4 3 2

To L & D and V & T
for the love of drawing
—SM

WISCONSIN, [REDACTED] HIGH SCHOOL GYMNASIUM, EARLY JUNE.

SARAH, 18, GRADUATING.

SARAH, GRADUATED.

EXIT

SARAH, THE REST OF LIFE.

THAT WAS IT?

KNOCK, KNOCK.

HEY, YOU.
SORRY WE HAD TO LEAVE A LITTLE EARLY. I COULDN'T TAKE THOSE BLEACHERS ANYMORE. AND GRANDPA NEEDED HIS NEBULIZER. I HOPE YOU DON'T MIND.

NAH. I MOSTLY JUST TALKED TO PEOPLE'S MOMS ANYWAY, Y'KNOW.

AH, OK, I DIDN'T MISS MUCH. SO WHAT'S NEXT ON THE SOCIAL SCHEDULE?

SOME BONFIRE GRADUATION PARTY WITH FINN AND EMMA.
APPARENTLY, THIS GUY'S HOUSE IS ON THE RIVER, AND THEY GOT CATERING FROM CHUCK'S.

ARE YOU SURE YOU DON'T WANT US TO HAVE A GRADUATION PARTY?

YEAH, I'M FINE GOING TO EVERYONE ELSE'S— IT'S MORE FUN THAT WAY.

IS FINN PICKING YOU UP?
YEAH, IN A COUPLE OF MINUTES. CAN YOU UNZIP ME?
PAT
PAT

PAH
ZIP!
WHEN WILL YOU BE BACK?

WELL, FINN INVITED ME AND EMMA TO SLEEP OVER TONIGHT, AND HE'LL HAVE TO DROP ME OFF BEFORE THEY BOTH GO TO WORK TOMORROW,
SO PROBABLY AROUND 8:30?

OK. JUST MAKE SURE YOU SPEND SOME TIME WITH YOUR BROTHER BEFORE YOU START WORK NEXT WEEK. AND PLEASE GET SOME SLEEP. I DON'T WANT THAT SINUS INFECTION TO FLARE UP AGAIN.

ALL RIGHT, ALL RIGHT.
I GOTTA GO WAIT OUTSIDE.

TEXT ME WHEN YOU GET TO FINN'S TONIGHT. YOU KNOW I DON'T LIKE YOU GUYS OUT DRIVING LATE.
SMECK

YEP.
LOVE YA.
BYE!

SIGH

LICK
LICK

FINN IS GONNA HELP ME FIND AN APARTMENT IN THE CITY AFTER MY PARENTS SELL THE HOUSE.
WE'RE TRANSFERRING TO THE HOLLANDER LOCATION DOWNTOWN, WHICH HAS MUCH BETTER TIPS.
AND I THINK I'LL GET MY BARTENDING LICENSE.
I WISH I COULD TAKE A GAP YEAR. I BET IT WOULD BE HARD TO GO BACK TO SCHOOL AFTER A BREAK, THOUGH.
MY PARENTS WOULD ***KILL*** ME IF I DIDN'T GO STRAIGHT TO COLLEGE.
I MEAN, I DON'T KNOW WHAT I'D STUDY IF I ***DID*** GO, SO WHY WASTE THE TIME AND RISK THE LOANS?

SARAH, WHERE ARE YOU GOING TO SCHOOL AGAIN?

M-M-MINNESOTA.

MY GRANDPA WENT TO MINNESOTA! I PROBABLY COULD HAVE GOTTEN A LEGACY SCHOLARSHIP, BUT LUCKILY I GOT INTO MY FIRST CHOICE—
BROWN'S PREMED PROGRAM.

NOT THAT THERE'S ANYTHING WRONG WITH MINNESOTA.

THANKS.

HAVE YOU PICKED YOUR MAJOR?

I THINK ENGLISH. I'M STILL CONSIDERING TRANSFERRING TO AN ART SCHOOL, BUT THEY'RE SO EXPENSIVE, AND I DON'T THINK I SHOULD COMMIT YET IF I'M NOT TOTALLY SET ON IT.

HUH, I WOULD'VE THOUGHT YOU WERE GOING TO DO THEATER, WITH ALL THE PLAYS AND STUFF.
OH, YEAH...I DON'T THINK I'M REALLY CUT OUT FOR THAT.

BROWN
BRANDON SMITH
ST HAIR
MOST LIKELY TO WIN AN OSCAR
JOHNSON
SARAH MAI
ST FLIRT
BEST SMILE

AMELIE, I HEARD YOU'RE HEAD STAFF AT CAMP THIS YEAR. THAT'S AWESOME!

THANKS! I ACTUALLY LEAVE IN TWO DAYS FOR A BACKPACKING TRIP IN THE PORCUPINES. I'M WITH THE BEAVER CABIN GROUP THIS YEAR, SO I THINK IT'LL BE FUN AND DIFFERENT...

IT'S GONNA BE SO WEIRD WITHOUT YOU HERE.
YEAH, LIKE, WHERE AM I SUPPOSED TO GET A FREE HAIRCUT NOW?

THANKS, FINN. THAT'S REALLY HEARTWARMING.
I'M KIDDING. YOU KNOW I LOVE YOU.

I FEEL KINDA GUILTY LEAVING YOU ALONE WITH THE APARTMENT AND EVERYTHING.

I MEAN...MY MOM COMES BACK OFTEN ENOUGH, SO IT'S NOT THAT BAD. PLUS, FINN IS OBSESSED WITH ME, SO I DON'T THINK I'LL ACTUALLY GET ENOUGH ALONE TIME.

HAHA

BOYFRIEND?

HAVE YOU HAD THE TALK YET?
OOF

UH...NOT REALLY. I'M TRYING TO NOT OVERTHINK EVERYTHING. I MEAN, WE STILL HAVE, LIKE, THREE MONTHS OF BLISSFUL AVOIDANCE, SO...EH?

OF COURSE.

I JUST WANT TO HAVE A NICE SUMMER BEFORE LEAVING. A COUPLE OF MONTHS OF ACTUALLY FEELING 18 FOR ONCE.

WE DESERVE IT.

WE'RE GONNA HAVE FUN THIS SUMMER, RIGHT, FINN?

HUH?

THE NEXT MORNING.

SUMMER JOB

JUNE AND JULY

DATE NIGHT.
I'M SO OUT OF BREATH. I CAN'T BELIEVE THIS THING IS SO HIGH.
IT'S GORGEOUS.
WE SHOULD COME HERE MORE OFTEN.
YEAH, WE SHOULD.
CLICK
AH!
NO, I'M SWEATY.
CLICK
YOU'RE BEAUTIFUL.
WE'RE GONNA GET CAUGHT IF WE DON'T LEAVE BEFORE DARK!
WE'RE NOT GONNA GET CAUGHT!

SARAH?
YEAH?
I THINK WE SHOULD TALK ABOUT THE FALL, BECAUSE...
I'M THE ONE LEAVING THE CITY, SO IT'S REALLY UP TO HOW YOU FEEL AND WHAT YOU WANT TO DO. I MEAN, I DON'T EVEN KNOW WHAT WE ARE.
BUT IT'S OK IF WE DON'T WANT TO LABEL ANYTHING—OR IF YOU WANT TO BREAK UP, TOO. IT'S FINE. I CAN HANDLE IT—
NO! I DON'T WANT TO—OF COURSE I WANT TO STAY TOGETHER. I WANT YOU TO BE MY GIRLFRIEND.
OH!
I WANT YOU TO BE MY GIRLFRIEND BECAUSE...

...BECAUSE
I LOVE YOU.
HE SAID WHAT?
HE TOLD ME
HE LOVED ME.

I DON'T KNOW, EMMA. WE HUGGED, AND THEN I SAID IT BACK. I WAS JUST A LITTLE SURPRISED. I MEAN, I KNOW WE REALLY LIKE EACH OTHER AND THINGS HAVE BEEN UNUSUALLY GOOD, BUT I DIDN'T THINK WHEN I ASKED IF WE WERE BREAKING UP, HIS RESPONSE WOULD BE, "NO, I *LOVE* YOU."

WELL, YOU KNOW HOW I GET WHEN THEY SMOKE AND STUFF, SO...
...I DON'T NEED TO BE THERE.
BE WHERE?
BEN TOLD ME HE LOVES ME LAST NIGHT.
CUTE.
WANT AIOLI?
THIS SIDE UP
FRAGILE
HANDLE WITH CARE
YOU KNOW WHAT? I AM SURE I LOVE HIM BACK. I AM READY FOR THIS.

WELL, GOOD, BECAUSE HE'S COMING TO SUMMERFEST WITH US, AND IT WOULD SUCK IF YOU TWO BROKE UP BEFORE THAT.

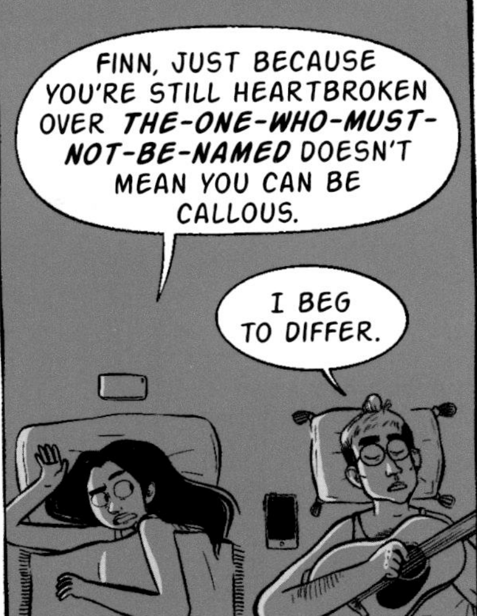
FINN, JUST BECAUSE YOU'RE STILL HEARTBROKEN OVER ***THE-ONE-WHO-MUST-NOT-BE-NAMED*** DOESN'T MEAN YOU CAN BE CALLOUS.
I BEG TO DIFFER.

BREAKUP BONFIRE, 3 MONTHS AGO.
TO BURN

WELL, I'LL HAVE PLENTY OF TIME TO THINK WHILE I'M UP NORTH. IT'LL BE GOOD.

ANNUAL FAMILY FISH-KILLING BONDING TIME.
NOT GOOD
NORTHERN WISCONSIN, JULY 1, UNSEASONABLY RAINY.
SO...
...
...
HOW'S BIG TOE DOING?
FINE. I'M TIRED.
BIG TOE
DO YOU WANT TO–
NO.

I KNOW! I KNOW! I'M STRESSED ABOUT GETTING EVERYTHING DONE BEFORE I LEAVE. I STILL HAVE TO PICK MY CLASSES, BUT THEY HAVE TO BE THE RIGHT ONES, BECAUSE IF NOT, I'LL FALL BEHIND IN MY GRADUATION PLAN, SO I SHOULD PICK MY MAJOR, WHICH WOULD HELP ME PICK CLASSES, BUT I'M NOT EVEN SURE I'M GOING TO THE SCHOOL THAT I'LL GRADUATE FROM, AND I NEED TO DO ALL THE ORIENTATION MODULES AND BUY EVERYTHING FOR THE DORM AND I HAVE TO PLANT, LIKE, 300 HOSTAS NEXT WEEK BEFORE THEY ROT, BUT I'M GOING TO SUMMERFEST WITH MY FRIENDS, EXCEPT I FEEL BAD FOR WASTING TIME, BECAUSE I JUST REALLY NEED TO FOCUS.

MID-JULY, SUMMERFEST.
YOU GOT SO TAN WHILE YOU WERE UP NORTH. IT LOOKS GOOD.
NO, THAT'S A SUNBURN.
ARE YOU SURE ABOUT THIS TOP? I FEEL LIKE MY BOOBS ARE FALLING OUT.
YOUR BOOBS ARE ICONIC. OK. ONE,
TWO,
THREE...
FLASH!
WHIZZZZ
SARAH + FINN

PARK AND RIDE SPECIAL
BRING CANNED GOODS FOR $5.00 TIX
FINN, ARE YOU READY TO GO?
PASSION PIT

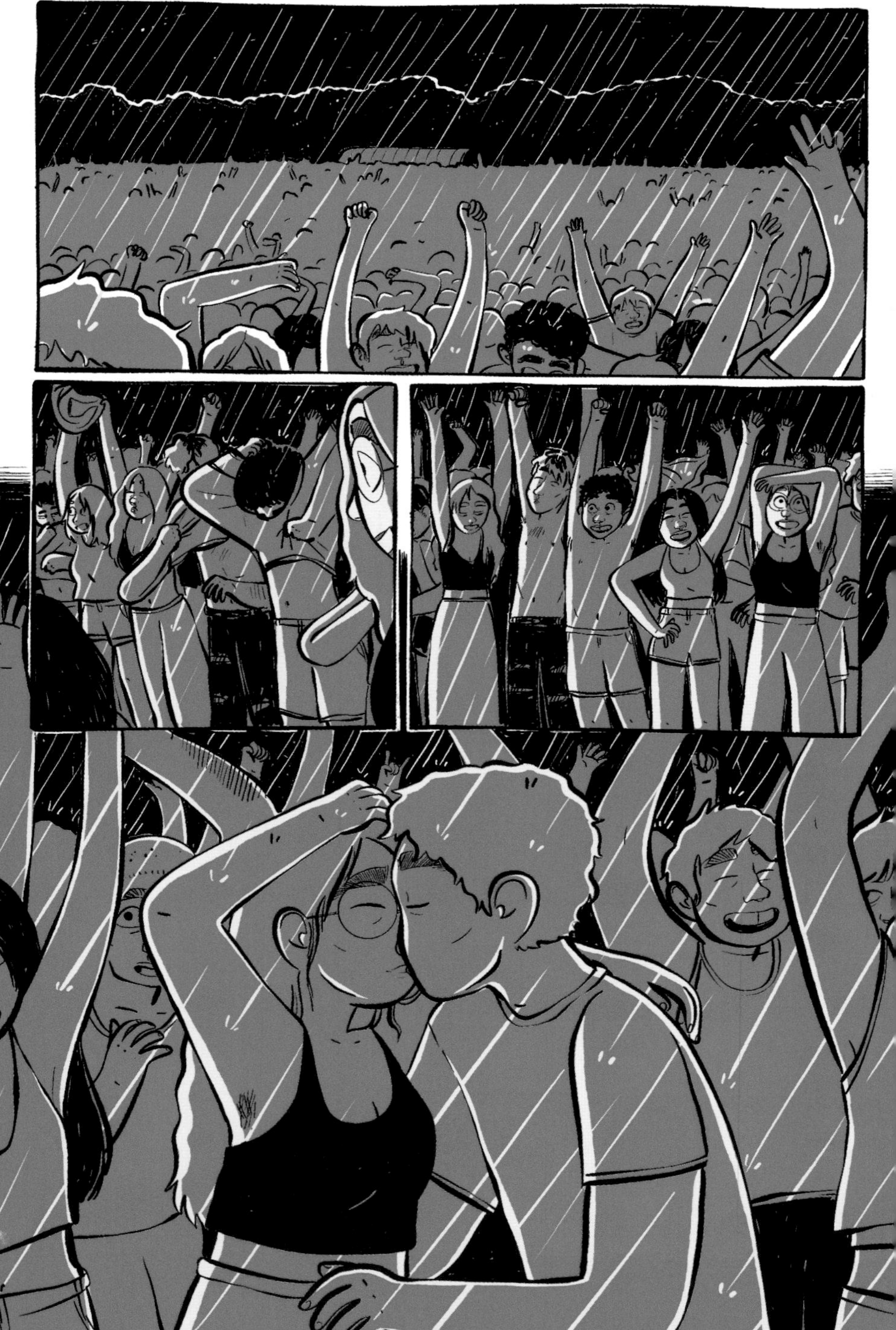

ALREADY MID-AUGUST, 7:00 A.M.
AGH
STILL WANT TO GO GET YOUR DORM STUFF THIS AFTERNOON?
DUVET SET
XL TWIN
home
HOME GOODS: HELL ON EARTH.
4:30 P.M.: RUSH HOUR IN HELL.
ARE YOU SURE YOU DON'T NEED THESE? IT COULD BE NICE TO START FRESH.
2 PACK ULTRA SOFT PILLOW CASES
WE HAVE A CLOSET FULL OF PILLOWCASES AT HOME, MOM. I ONLY NEED TWO: ONE TO USE, ONE TO WASH. ALSO, I THINK THOSE ARE FROM THE CHILDREN'S SECTION.
OK, OK...I'M JUST GOING TO HANG ON TO THEM FOR NOW.

THIS LIST IS SO EXCESSIVE. AN ALARM CLOCK? WHAT DECADE IS IT?

WOMENS' F
ARE YOU SURE YOU DON'T WANT TO LOOK AT THE SLACKS? I SAW SOME CUTE ONES OVER BY THE SWEATERS. MIGHT BE NICE IF YOU HAVE AN INTERVIEW OR SOMETHING.

SLACKS. EYUGH. I HATE THAT WORD.
EYUGH. I HATE THOSE PANTS.

REMEMBER THE OUTFITS YOU USED TO WEAR? THOSE LITTLE PEDAL PUSHERS AND THE CUTE SWEATERS? I MISS WHEN YOU DRESSED LIKE THAT.

SARAH AT 14.
UNIQUE AWARD
I'M NOT LIKE OTHER GIRLS!!!
SO QUIRKY!
WOW, CONGRATS!

IT'S NOT REALLY...
MY LOOK ANYMORE.

DID YOU MESSAGE LIZ ABOUT THE MINIFRIDGE AND MICROWAVE?
MOM, YOU ASKED ME THAT THIS MORNING.

OH.
WHAT WAS THE ANSWER AGAIN?
SHE'S PICKING UP BOTH FROM HER AUNT'S HOUSE ON THE WAY TO MINNESOTA.

OH, OK. SORRY.
MY MEMORY.

HMMM...

SIGH

I'M JUST GOING TO CLOSE MY EYES FOR A MINUTE.
FEELING A LITTLE NAUSEOUS.

PLANNER
2016-17

OK, I THINK I'M READY.

HMM? READY?
YEAH.

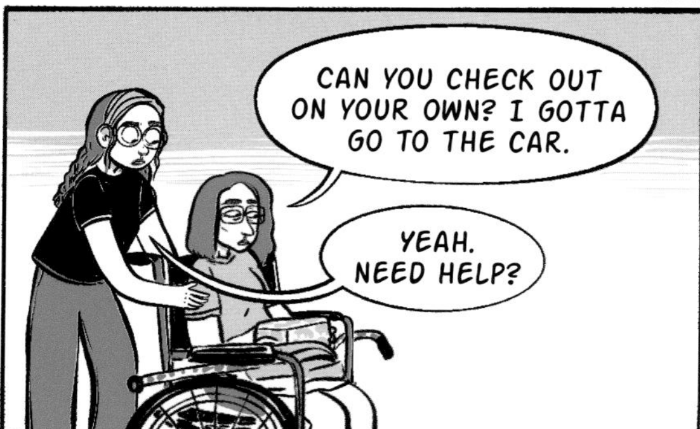
CAN YOU CHECK OUT ON YOUR OWN? I GOTTA GO TO THE CAR.
YEAH. NEED HELP?

NO, NO.

FINN'S HAVING A POETRY SESH AT HIS HOUSE TONIGHT, SO I THINK I'M GOING TO DO THAT LATER IF THAT'S OK.
MM-HMM.
GOOD MOM
BAD DAUGHTER
THANKS, MOM. FOR THE...STUFF.
BLINK BLINK
YOUR GRANDMA DROVE ME NUTS WHEN I WAS YOUR AGE. I WANTED TO GO FAAAAR AWAY.
BUT I WAS HAPPY TO BE HOME BY THANKSGIVING.

POETRY SESH, PRETTY MUCH OVER.

YOU GUYS ARE SO LUCKY YOU DON'T HAVE TO DO THIS RIGHT NOW.

THE EFFECTS OF CANNABIS ON THE ADOLESCENT BRAIN

NEXT

DO YOU THINK ANY OF THAT HAS EVER ACTUALLY STOPPED PEOPLE FROM DOING DRUGS WHEN THEY GO TO COLLEGE? IF YOU'RE THE KIND OF PERSON WHO WANTS TO EXPERIMENT, YOU DO IT, AND IF YOU'RE NOT, YOU DON'T.

I MEAN, I KNOW I'M NEVER GOING TO SMOKE. WHY WOULD THEY NEED TO BEAT IT INTO MY SKULL?

THE BAR IS SO LOW.

IT'S LIKE D.A.R.E. ALL OVER AGAIN. I CAN'T BELIEVE I GOT ROPED INTO TEACHING THAT. I DON'T THINK IT EVEN MATTERED ON MY APPLICATIONS...

...AND IT MAKES ME LOOK LIKE A NARC.

YOU'RE RIGHT— IT DOES MAKE YOU LOOK LIKE A NARC.

BONK

I JUST THINK THEY SHOULD TEACH US THAT IT'S OK TO BE CURIOUS,
AS LONG AS WE ARE RESPECTFUL OF OUR BODIES AND TREAT OURSELVES WITH KINDNESS.
I WISH.
BITE
IT'S A LITTLE HARD TO DEFINE SELF-RESPECT AND KINDNESS VIA MULTIPLE-CHOICE QUIZZES.
CLICK
BITE
CLICK
NUBS
THERE GOES MY LAST FINGERNAIL.

ONE WEEK BEFORE THE GREAT MOVE OUT.
PISSSSSSSSsss
OH CRAP!
DAD, HUEY JUST PEED ON MY LAUNDRY BASKET.
DID YOU NOT TAKE HIM OUT?
IS SOMEONE CALLING ME?
I FORGOT; I'VE BEEN A LITTLE PREOCCUPIED.

GRUNT

WELL, HE HAS TO PEE SOMEWHERE IF HE DOESN'T GET TAKEN OUTSIDE.
ALL RIGHT, ALL RIGHT.

HEY! WHAT ARE YOU UP TO?
NOTHING, JUST...

...NOTHING.

WANNA GO GET FROYO AND DRIVE AROUND?
I CAN'T. MY BROTHER'S MAKING BRATS TONIGHT, SO MY PARENTS WANT ME TO BE HERE.

OH.

THINK THERE'S ENOUGH FOR ME?

SO, FINN, YOUR MOM TOLD ME YOU'RE DOING A GAP YEAR.
POTATO SALAD SUPREME

MM-HMM...EMMA AND I ARE GONNA WORK AT THE NEW HOLLANDER THEY OPENED DOWNTOWN. THEY NEED ALL-NEW STAFF, AND WE'RE ALREADY TRAINED, SO WE'LL GET PAID MORE.

NEXT YEAR, I THINK I'M GONNA MOVE TO NEW YORK AND STUDY COMPOSITION AT THE NEW SCHOOL.

LIKE, MUSIC COMPOSITION?
YEP. CLASSICAL MUSIC COMPOSITION.

WHAT ARE YOU GOING TO DO WITH *THAT?*
ROB.

NAH, IT'S COOL.
I MIGHT TEACH MUSIC OR MAYBE START A BAND. VINNY LIVES OUT THERE NOW, SO I WILL PROBABLY JUST MOVE IN WITH HIM AND FIGURE IT OUT. I DON'T KNOW—MAYBE I'LL END UP IN FASHION OR SOMETHING.

YOU DON'T HAVE TO STUDY THE THING YOU WANT TO DO FOR A JOB; I DON'T THINK IT'S THAT IMPORTANT.
UNLESS YOU WANT TO BE AN ENGINEER.
ARE YOU SARAH'S BOYFRIEND?

I DON'T KNOW WHY EVERYONE ALWAYS THINKS WE'RE DATING.
BITE?
WE'D BE A TERRIBLE COUPLE.
YEAH. NO OFFENSE; I WOULDN'T DATE YOU.
HA. WE'D KILL EACH OTHER.
I THINK I'M GONNA MISS THIS THE MOST.
THE CORN?
JUST...
EVERYTHING.
OH.

MOST OF HIGH SCHOOL WAS GARBAGE ANYWAY. I MEAN... WHY DO YOU THINK WE'RE ALWAYS DRIVING AROUND TALKING ABOUT OUR FEELINGS?

WELL, YEAH, I'M NOT GONNA MISS ALL THAT...

SARAH'S HIGH SCHOOL EMOTIONAL LANDSCAPE

AHHHHH! GOD HAS FORSAKEN US!

I ALWAYS HAVE YOU AND EMMA WHEN I NEED TO GET AWAY FROM EVERYTHING, YOU KNOW? IT JUST MAKES ME SO SAD TO THINK I WON'T HAVE YOU GUYS AROUND. IT WON'T BE THE SAME.
YEAH.
IT WON'T.
WANT TO GO WALK AROUND MEIJER?
OK.

LATE AUGUST, MOVING DAY.
SMOOCH

HERE

NICE.

...THAT'S HOW THE DRUMMER OF LED ZEPPELIN DIED. SO IF YOU SEE SOMEONE WHO IS TOO DRUNK, PUT THEM ON THEIR SIDE IN THE LATERAL RECUMBENT POSITION.

YEAH, I KNOW, DAD.

TERRIBLE THINGS THAT COULD HAPPEN

CHECK-IN #1
CAN YOU TELL DAD TO, LIKE, RELAX A LITTLE BIT? HE'S FREAKING EVERYBODY OUT.
I THINK HE JUST NEEDS TO GET THIS OUT OF HIS SYSTEM.
SUPER ABSORBANT
JUMBO PADS
FOR YOUR HUGE, SCARY PERIOD
SPECIAL DISCREET PACKAGE
BIG HUGE PADS
HIGH DOSE ESTROGEN BIRTH CONTROL
EXTRA STRENGTH RASH OINTMENT
THUD
BE CAREFUL—YOUR LAPTOP'S IN THERE.

MOVE-IN DAY
CHECKLIST:
OVER HERE?
NO, BY THE ELECTRICAL OUTLET.
BE CAREFUL WITH THAT!
WELCOME!
HI!
MINNESOTA MOM
YOU MUST BE SARAH!
CAN I GIVE YOU A HUG? I'M A HUGGER.
MINNESOTA MOM
AND PARENTS, HI! I'M RACHEL. THIS IS JOHN, MARCUS, SEBASTIAN, KATIE, AND MY SISTER JUDIE. AND OF COURSE, LIZ.
HEY!

WOW, YOU'RE ALREADY SET UP HERE! WHERE'S ALL MY STUFF GONNA GO? HEH HEH.

WE CAN EITHER HELP YOU UNPACK OR GET OUT OF THE WAY.
WHAT WOULD BE BEST?
MINNESOTA MOM

WE ARE GONNA GET OUT OF THE WAY.
I HAVE EXTRA DINING PASSES ON MY MEAL PLAN, SO LET'S GRAB SOME LUNCH AND LEAVE THEM ALONE.

OH, IT'S OK–
TRUST ME.

BYE.
BYE.
BYE.
BYE.
BYE.
HI.
BYE.

THEY SEEM NICE! THOSE BOYS ARE ADORABLE.
DO I NEED TO MOVE THE CAR? AM I GOING TO GET TOWED WHERE I'M PARKED?

NO, DAD, THOSE SPOTS ARE BLOCKED OFF FOR MOVE-IN. IT'S FINE.
THIS BED LOOKS PRETTY HARD. SHOULD WE GO TO COSTCO AND GET YOU A MATTRESS TOPPER?

LET'S JUST START WITH UNPACKING THE CART.
I'M GOING TO GO DOUBLE-CHECK ON THE CAR.

KILL ME NOW.

MOM...HOW MUCH STUFF DID YOU SNEAK IN HERE?
TWIN XL SHEETS

I DON'T KNOW, A COUPLE OF THINGS.

IS THE CAR INTACT?

HA. HA.
WE SHOULD HEAD OUT SOON IF WE'RE GOING TO MAKE IT BACK BEFORE RUSH HOUR.

OK, OK. I JUST WANT A PICTURE WITH MY LITTLE GIRL BEFORE WE GO.

HAVE A GOOD SEMESTER, OK?

OK.

ALL GROWN UP.
BE GOOD.
SMOOTCH

CLICK

SCROLL
HELLO?
OH, HEY, SORRY.
DON'T WORRY– NOBODY ELSE IS COMING IN. MY FAMILY JUST TOOK OFF.
OH, COOL.
SO HOW WAS THE DRIVE?
MINUS MY BROTHERS SCREAMING AND CRYING THE WHOLE WAY HERE, PRETTY GOOD.
I CRIED THE WHOLE WAY HERE.
SCARED OF LADDERS
NICE, NICE.
THANKS FOR PICKING UP THE MINIFRIDGE AND STUFF.
NO PROBLEM! IT WAS ALREADY ON THE WAY.

COOL...
DO YOU WANNA GRAB SOME DINNER?
YOU HUNGRY?
STARVING. LET'S GET OUT OF HERE.
I HOPE THEY HAVE CHICKEN NUGGETS.
AFTER DINNER.
WELL, WE DID IT!
LOOKS GREAT! I LOVE IT.

ONLY THE ESSENTIALS
WELL, I SHOULD PROBABLY GET TO BED. IT'S GONNA BE A LONG DAY TOMORROW.
10:37 pm
MY GRANDPA DOESN'T EVEN GO TO BED AT 10:30.
DO WE HAVE ALL THE SAME EVENTS THIS WEEK?
YEAH! I THINK EVERYTHING'S THE SAME EXCEPT FOR A FEW BREAKOUT GROUPS FOR THE ENGINEERING SCHOOL, BUT WE SHOULD SIT TOGETHER FOR THE REST OF THE PRESENTATIONS.
PTEW
SPLAT

11:00 P.M.
I JUST REALIZED THAT NOW WE'RE JUST... HERE. I SIGNED UP TO DO THIS, AND THEN MY PARENTS DROPPED ME OFF, AND NOW WE'RE HERE, AND NOW I AM DOING IT.
UH...UH-HUH...
I JUST PUT ALL THIS STUFF IN A CAR AND DROVE HERE, AND NOW I LIVE IN THIS ROOM, AND IT'S POSSIBLE THAT I WON'T LIVE AT HOME... PROBABLY FOR, LIKE...EVER AGAIN.
YEP.
CLICK
WELL, ANYWAY... GOOD NIGHT!
MIDNIGHT.

THE NEXT MORNING, 7:15.
Zzzz
ARE YOU TWO HERE FOR THE PRESENTATION? AUDITORIUM IS THROUGH THOSE SILVER DOORS.
HAVE FUN!
HEHE HEHE

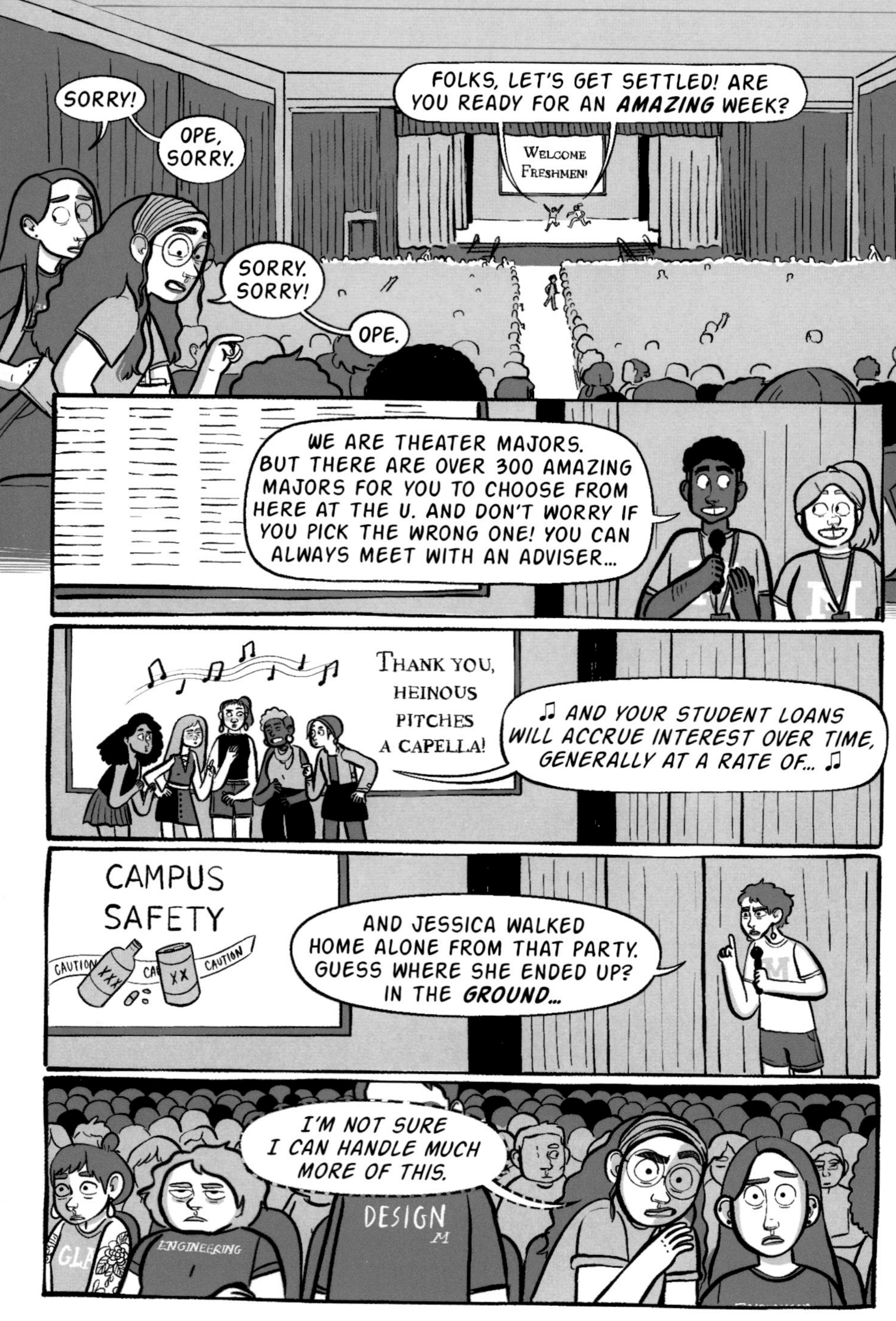
SORRY!
OPE, SORRY.
FOLKS, LET'S GET SETTLED! ARE YOU READY FOR AN *AMAZING* WEEK?
WELCOME FRESHMEN!
SORRY. SORRY!
OPE.
WE ARE THEATER MAJORS. BUT THERE ARE OVER 300 AMAZING MAJORS FOR YOU TO CHOOSE FROM HERE AT THE U. AND DON'T WORRY IF YOU PICK THE WRONG ONE! YOU CAN ALWAYS MEET WITH AN ADVISER...
THANK YOU, HEINOUS PITCHES A CAPELLA!
♫ AND YOUR STUDENT LOANS WILL ACCRUE INTEREST OVER TIME, GENERALLY AT A RATE OF... ♫
CAMPUS SAFETY
CAUTION
CAUTION
XXX
XX
AND JESSICA WALKED HOME ALONE FROM THAT PARTY. GUESS WHERE SHE ENDED UP? IN THE *GROUND*...
I'M NOT SURE I CAN HANDLE MUCH MORE OF THIS.
DESIGN
ENGINEERING

THREE HOURS LATER.
BOOM BOOM CLAP, MARVELOUS MICHAEL, BOOM BOOM CLAP, CAREFUL CANDICE, BOOM BOOM CLAP...
GROUP ACTIVI
DON'T TRY TOO HARD. SAY, LIKE, SILLY SARAH OR SOMETHING.
BOOM BOOM CLAP, DOUBTFUL DAVID, BOOM BOOM CLAP, PARTY PAUL, BOOM BOOM...
...CLAP.
OH SHIT.
BOOM BOOM CLAP, OH SHIT SARAH, BOOM BOOM...

I CAN'T BELIEVE I INTRODUCED MYSELF AS "OH SHIT SARAH." I'LL DISSOLVE IF I EVER SEE ANY OF THOSE PEOPLE AGAIN.

GLA

THERE'S, LIKE, TENS OF THOUSANDS OF PEOPLE ON CAMPUS. I BET YOU WON'T EVER SEE THEM AGAIN. I MEAN, IT'S KIND OF FUNNY ANYWAY.

GROAN

OH SHIT SARAH! HEY!

GLA

GLA

WHAT'S YOUR MAJOR?
WHAT'S YOUR MAJOR?
WHAT'S YOUR MAJOR?
WHAT'S YOUR MAJOR?
POOF!
YOU'VE NEVER HAD TOP THE TATER?!
YOU NEED TO RUSH. GREEK LIFE IS CRITICAL FOR STARTING A CAREER.
WELL, ACTUALLY, I WAS THE THIRD PERSON IN MY SCHOOL TO EVER GET A PERFECT SCORE ON THE A.C.T.
ZZZZ
WE MEET ON WEDNESDAYS, FRIDAYS, AND SUNDAYS, AND SOMETIMES MONDAYS.
WAH WAH WAH WAH WAH. WAH WAH WAH. WAH WAH.
SO I KNOW WE'RE BOTH POOPED, BUT DO YOU WANT TO MEET MY FRIEND MADDY AT THE STATE FAIR TOMORROW? WE WENT TO MIDDLE AND HIGH SCHOOL TOGETHER. I THINK YOU'D LIKE HER.

HONEY OF THE MIDWEST

IT'S GREAT TO FINALLY MEET YOU! LIZ'S TOLD ME ALL ABOUT YOU!

SO, DO YOU GUYS WANT TO CHECK OUT THE COOKIE-BUCKET STAND?

I'M SUPPOSED TO WRITE AN ARTICLE ABOUT IT. I GUESS IT'S FAMOUS.

I DIDN'T KNOW YOU COULD WORK ON CAMPUS BEFORE SCHOOL OFFICIALLY STARTED.

YEAH, I'M DOUBLE MAJORING IN ENGLISH AND THEATER.
THAT'S AWESOME! I THINK I'M LEANING TOWARD ENGLISH, BUT...I'M NOT TOTALLY SURE YET. I USED TO DO A LOT OF THEATER, BUT NOW I'M KIND OF BURNED OUT ON THE WHOLE THING.

SIX MONTHS AGO

MADDY AND I WERE IN *HAIRSPRAY* TOGETHER LAST YEAR. SHE WAS TRACY. I WAS THAT ONE CHARACTER WHO GOT PREGNANT.

OH MY GOD, *LIZ*, JACK FOUND A RECORDING OF IT ONLINE. HE SENT IT TO ME LAST WEEK.

I DON'T THINK I COULD EVER WATCH IT AGAIN.
IF I CAN SIT THROUGH IT, YOU CAN, TOO.

BUZZT

BEN
SM
Miss you already!
Hope you're having fun!
Love you <3
EVERYTHING GOOD?
OH, YEAH, IT'S JUST BEN.
WHO'S BEN?
MY, UH, BOYFRIEND.
JUST CHECKING IN.
CHEW CHEW
B
BEN
Miss you already!
Hope you're having fun!
Love you <3
B
Love you too,
I'll call you later :)
SM

MY STOMACH IS KILLING ME. I THINK I'M LACTOSE INTOLERANT.
GURGLE GURGLE
PROBABLY.
MOST PEOPLE ARE.
I LIKE MADDY A LOT, BY THE WAY.
YEAH, SHE'S GREAT.
WE'RE GOING TO THE UNION TOMORROW TO PICK UP OUR TEXTBOOKS, IF YOU WANT TO COME.
I THOUGHT THEY WERE GONNA GIVE US LISTS IN OUR FIRST CLASSES THIS WEEK.
OH. MY PROFESSORS EMAILED THE LISTS TO ME TWO WEEKS AGO.
PTEW!
WE HAVE EMAILS?

FLASH!
Sarah Mai
ID: 12345689
STUDENT PASS
AT LEAST THE NUMBER IS MEMORABLE.

AND THEN I HAVE THE *VAGINA MONOLOGUES* FOR MY WOMEN: PROTESTERS, POETS, AND PRISONERS FRESHMAN SEMINAR. THE PROFESSOR USUALLY TEACHES SENIOR THESIS GROUPS, BUT SHE DECIDED TO DO A SEMINAR THIS YEAR, TOO.

I THOUGHT THEY JUST WANTED US TO TAKE FRESHMAN SEMINARS SO WE COULD STAY OUT OF THE WAY OF PEOPLE DOING THEIR GRADUATION-REQUIREMENT CLASSES.

IT'S SO YOU CAN TALK TO SENIOR FACULTY BEFORE YOU'RE AN UPPERCLASSMAN. IF YOU TOOK A BUNCH OF A.P.S, YOU DON'T HAVE TO DO THOSE BASIC INTRO CLASSES ANYWAY, LIKE ALGEBRA AND SPANISH OR WHATEVER.

I TOOK SOME A.P.S...BUT I STILL HAVE TO DO MY MATH AND SCIENCE CREDITS, AND A LANGUAGE. I DID SPANISH IN HIGH SCHOOL, JUST NOT A.P. I DIDN'T REALIZE THAT WAS GOING TO BE A PROBLEM...
YEAH, LANGUAGE REQUIREMENTS ARE FOUR SEMESTERS. AND THEY'RE EVERY DAY OF THE WEEK.

DUDE, I SIGNED UP FOR FRENCH. OH MY GOD.

NO, IT'S COOL, THOUGH. YOU'LL BE TRILINGUAL BY THE TIME YOU'RE OUT OF COLLEGE. I HEARD IT HELPS TO STUDY FRENCH WHEN YOU'RE AN ENGLISH MAJOR SINCE A LOT OF OLD ENGLISH IS BASICALLY FRENCH.
THANK GOD FOR THE NORMAN INVASION.

WHAT ELSE ARE YOU TAKING?
UH... HANG ON...

FRENCH, CREATIVE WRITING, DRAWING, AND TEXTUAL ANALYSIS METHODS.
1:17
CREATIVE WRIT
INTRO TO DRAW.
OH, AND THAT ONLINE FRESHMAN EXPERIENCE CREDIT, OR WHATEVER IT'S CALLED.

THAT SOUNDS LIKE A FUN SCHEDULE TO ME.
WAY BETTER THAN MINE.

WELL, IT'S JUST THE FIRST SEMESTER. I CAN GET SETTLED AND TAKE MORE CHALLENGING CLASSES IN THE SPRING.
PROBABLY.

FIRST WEEK OF CLASS.
Top 10 Majors That Guarantee Jobs
1. ENGINEERING
I REALLY FELT I BELONGED WHEN I LIVED IN BARTHELONA FOR FIVE MONTHS. YOU'VE NEVER TASTED FOOD UNTIL YOU'VE HAD AUTHENTIC PAELLA–SIMPLY INCREDIBLE.
I WANT TO GO LIVE IN MARSEILLE NEXT YEAR, REALLY SOAK IN THE VINO CULTURE.
NOD
OH!
BONJOUR À TOUS. JE M'APPELLE FARIDA. BIENVENUE AU PREMIER JOUR DU COURS DE FRANÇAIS.
POUR DÉBUTER, NOUS ALLONS APPRENDRE QUELQUES EXPRESSIONS DE BASE.
VEUILLEZ OUVRIR VOS LIVRES À LA PAGE QUINZE.
FLIP FLIP FLIP
QUINZE?
SHRUG
CHUCKLE

CREATIVE WRITING LECTURE.
PROBLEMS THAT CAN BE RESOLVED WITH DIALOGUE ARE NOT BIG ENOUGH!
REMEMBER, MR. VOLDEMORT AND MR. POTTER'S RELATIONSHIP WAS NOT FIXED WITH COUPLE'S THERAPY!
CREATIVE WRITING DISCUSSION.
TODAY WE ARE GOING TO ANALYZE LYRICS BY KENDRICK LAMAR. I KNOW WHAT YOU'RE THINKING, BUT A SONG THAT IS A TOTAL BANGER CAN ALSO BE LITERATURE.

DRAWING.
THESE ARE NOT OBJECTS—THEY ARE VALUES. PLEASE TAKE OUT YOUR PENCILS AND PRACTICE SHADING ACCORDING TO THE CHART, FROM H TO 9B. LATER, WE WILL PRACTICE THE SAME BUT WITH CROSS-HATCHING.

SCRATCH
SCRATCH
SCRATCH
SCRATCH

GURGLE GURGLE

TEXTUAL ANALYSIS METHODS.
LIT METHODS
MATT HE/HIM
SO WHAT DO WE THINK ABOUT THE READING? WAS SOCRATES A TROLL?

FRIDAY NIGHT.
I THINK I HAVE A CRUSH ON MY T.A.
IS THAT BAD?
TAP TAP TAP
NO, THAT'S PART OF THE QUINTESSENTIAL COLLEGE EXPERIENCE. I LOVE MY ITALIAN LIT PROFESSOR.
HE'S LIKE A BIG LINGUINE NOODLE.
IF I HAVE TO WATCH ANOTHER TED TALK, I'M GOING TO THROW MY LAPTOP OUT THE WINDOW.
SO...MY ROOMMATE IS BEING INDUCTED INTO HER SORORITY TONIGHT, AND I KINDA DON'T WANT TO BE HOME UNTIL I KNOW SHE'S ASLEEP. IS THAT OK WITH YOU GUYS?
YOU COULD SLEEP OVER IF YOU WANT.
YEAH. HOW IS SHE?
Y'KNOW, A ROOMMATE. SHE KEEPS ORDERING NEW OUTFITS FOR EVERY SORORITY EVENT AND LEAVING TRASH ALL OVER THE ROOM. SHE SAID SHE'S GETTING ALL OF HER COLLEGE EXPERIENCE IN NOW BECAUSE SHE'S GRADUATING EARLY SINCE SHE DID THAT P.S.E.O. THING.
WHAT THE HELL IS P.S.E.O.?

IT'S LIKE EARLY COLLEGE. I WISH WISCONSIN HAD THAT.
FLIP

I SAW SOME PICTURES OF HER FROM HIGH SCHOOL ONLINE, AND IT'S SHOCKING HOW DIFFERENT SHE ALREADY IS. SHE'S LIKE A TOTALLY NEW PERSON.
HOW?

HER MOM POSTED A PICTURE LAST YEAR OF HER WINNING FIRST PLACE AT A DEBATE AND FORENSICS NATIONALS MEET, AND SHE WAS WEARING A MATCHING KNEE-LENGTH SKIRT AND BLAZER. LAST NIGHT, SHE THREW UP JUNGLE JUICE ON THE BATHROOM FLOOR AND LOST HER SHOES AT A PARTY. IT'S JUST A RADICALLY DIFFERENT VIBE.

LIZ, DID YOU STALK ME BEFORE WE MOVED IN TOGETHER?
OF COURSE.
OK, GOOD. ME TOO.

I BET HER PARENTS WERE REALLY STRICT OR SOMETHING. SHE'S TRYING ON A NEW IDENTITY.
MAYBE.

PATHS FOR HIGH SCHOOL OVERACHIEVERS IN COLLEGE
PRELAW
FAMOUS?
PARTY HARD
PREMED
GRAD SCHOOL
BUSINESS
TOTAL MELTDOWN
ENGINEER
DROP OUT
PREMONEY
RIP

BUZZ
BUZZ
BUZZ
BUZZ

AH! DO YOU MIND IF I TAKE THIS? IT'S MY FRIEND FROM HOME.
YEAH! AS LONG AS I CAN SAY HI.
BUZZ BUZZ BUZZ

YAAAYYY, SARAH PICKED UP!
HEY, FLOP!

WHERE ARE YOU? WHAT ARE YOU DOING?
JUST HANGING OUT IN THE DORM. THIS IS MADDY AND LIZ.

HEYYY, LIZ. WE STALKED YOU ON FACEBOOK. MADDY, I LOVE YOUR HAIR.
WHY, THANK YOU.
WHAT ARE YOU GUYS UP TO TONIGHT?
WE'RE ABOUT TO HEAD OUT TO *ROCKY HORROR*. WE'RE JUST AT BEN'S RIGHT NOW, BUT WE WANTED TO SAY HI BEFORE WE WENT OUT. IT'S SO WEIRD WITHOUT YOU. WE MISS YOU!
I MISS YOU GUYS, TOO. WHERE'S BEN?
HE'S GETTING SOMETHING FROM HIS CAR, I THINK.

AW. TELL HIM I MISS HIM. I CAN'T WAIT UNTIL YOU VISIT! IT'LL BE SO FUN.
I KNOW! EEE! OH, SHOOT, WE'RE ALREADY RUNNING LATE. I'LL CALL YOU LATER!
OK, BYE! LOVE YOU GUYS.
SORRY ABOUT THAT.
NO, THAT WAS FUN—THEY SEEM REALLY COOL. WHERE DID YOU MEET THEM?

I ALWAYS HAD OLDER FRIENDS, AND THEN THEY'D GRADUATE AND I'D HAVE TO START OVER THE NEXT YEAR, WHICH WAS FINE, I GUESS.

11-12 Bible Trivia Team

12-13 Catholic School Outcasts

13-14 Rec Department Theatre

14-15 Hipsters with Cameras

16-17 Stage Crew

17-18 Forever Friends?

Museum of Sarahthropology

SOCIAL ~~BUTTERFLY~~ ~~MOTH~~ LEECH

I'M CURIOUS ABOUT THIS MYSTERIOUS BEN. DO YOU HAVE A PIC?
HE'S ATHLETIC. Y'KNOW, LACROSSE AND STUFF.
WE'RE PRETTY DIFFERENT, BUT SOMEHOW IT WORKS.
HE'S CUTE. HOW'S THAT GOING?
IT'S KINDA HARD, BUT WE TALK ON THE PHONE A LOT, SO I THINK EVERYTHING'S GONNA BE ALL RIGHT!
ANYWAYS, DID YOU STILL WANT TO WATCH SOMETHING AT MY DORM ON WEDNESDAY?
OF COURSE!
CAN I JUST HANG OUT AND NOT WATCH? I ALREADY HAVE 15 CHEM MODULES...

SOIXANTE-QUATRE, SOIXANTE-CINQ, SOIXANTE-SIX, SOIXANTE-SEPT, SOIXANTE-HUIT...
WE'RE WEARING THE SAME SHOES.
HUH?
WE HAVE THE SAME EXACT SANDALS.
OH! HA, COOL.
BIRKENSTOCK BITCHES!
MY CREDITS DIDN'T TRANSFER OVER 'CAUSE THE SCHOOL IS OUTSIDE THE UNIVERSITY SYSTEM, WHICH SUCKS, BUT I'D RATHER TAKE FRENCH THAN BE IN MANKATO FOR ANOTHER TWO YEARS. PLUS, THEY DIDN'T HAVE MUCH OF AN ARTS SCENE, OR A QUEER SCENE, FOR THAT MATTER.
THAT'S ESSENTIALLY A VENN DIAGRAM THAT'S A CIRCLE.

MINE'S A WHOLE LONG THING WITH EIGHTH GRADE AND A SINUS INFECTION AND A.P. CREDITS...

IT REALLY DOESN'T MATTER.

SO YOU'RE A FRESHMAN? I WOULDN'T HAVE GUESSED THAT.

WHY, BECAUSE I'M NOT WEARING A LANYARD?

THAT'S...NICE OF YOU TO SAY. I'M STILL FIGURING OUT THE BUS ROUTES.

HEY, WELL, I HAVE TO HEAD OFF TO THE OTHER SIDE OF CAMPUS, BUT I'LL SEE YOU IN CLASS TOMORROW.

MADDY INVITED US OVER SATURDAY NIGHT. I KNOW YOU SAID YOU THOUGHT YOUR FRIENDS WERE GONNA COME VISIT THIS WEEKEND, BUT YOU'RE STILL INVITED.
Un(e) ami(e)
Un copain, un copine
Petit(e) ami(e)
FREE CLEAR
OH, YEAH...THEY HAD TO CANCEL SINCE BEN HAS A THING FOR SCHOOL AND EMMA AND FINN CAN'T GET THEIR SHIFTS CHANGED.
NO, MOM, I HAVE THE PODS... NO, DETERGENT PODS. HOW MANY DO I PUT IN THE MACHINE? AND THEN WHAT SETTING DO I DO? T-SHIRTS...
NO, TEE-SHIRTS.
SATURDAY NIGHT FEVER (AND CHILLS).

SWIPE
CLICK
OUR BUILDING IS LIKE A RETIREMENT COMMUNITY. OH MY GOD. WHAT IS IN THE WATER HERE?
CLINK CLINK CLINK CLINK
GRAPEFRUIT VODKA.
BEUUUURK!
AMY B
BETH J
JOE P
DANNY K
MADDY F
LANA S
403
CALLIE N
HUY T
401
311

Lady Bird
LADY GAGA COULD STEP ON ME AND I'D THANK HER.
notnotzachary 1 hr ago
TAP
WHAT'S UP?
NOTHING. JUST, NOTHING.
IT'S ALL GOOD.
VODKA
GLUG GLUG GLUG
GLUG
DOES ANYONE WANT TO SEE MY IMPRESSION OF A KID AUDITIONING FOR *ANNIE*?

HEYYYY.
HEY!
YOU MADE IT.
JUST BARELY.
ROUGH NIGHT?
YOU COULD SAY THAT.
I GET IT.
SO, DO WE KNOW WHAT FARIDA IS PUTTING ON THE QUIZ?
FOR VOCABULAIRE, I THINK IT'S BODY PARTS, AND FOR GRAMMAIRE, PRÉSENT AND IMPARFAIT.

HOW DO YOU SAY "I'M HOLLOW INSIDE" IN FRENCH?
PING!

B
Yesterday at 12:45 AM
i mis hou so mscuh
I live you <333
SM
Today at 2:17 PM
hey ily 2!
B

SORRY, DISTRACTED. UH...
BOYFRIEND?

I'VE HAD A FEW FRIENDS IN LONG-DISTANCE RELATIONSHIPS. I KNOW THAT LOOK.

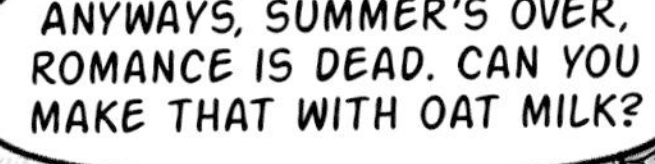

CASH ONLY
TEA DRINKS
ANYWAYS, SUMMER'S OVER, ROMANCE IS DEAD. CAN YOU MAKE THAT WITH OAT MILK?

WHO KNEW CHICKEN COULD BE SO...GRAY?

I THINK I SEE SOME KIND OF GRAIN BOWL THING OVER THERE, BUT I'M NOT ACTUALLY SURE.

AND THE VEGETARIAN OPTION TONIGHT IS LITERAL SLOP. I THOUGHT OUR DINING HALL WAS SUPPOSED TO BE GOOD? OR IS THIS JUST WHAT HAPPENS TO THE FOOD AFTER THE FIRST MONTH?

MAYBE THE KITCHEN STAFF IS RETALIATING FOR HOW IRRITATING IT MUST BE TO OPEN ALL THOSE BIG CANS EVERY DAY.

SOMEONE IN MY CHEM STUDY GROUP SAID THAT THE DORM DOWN THE STREET WHERE ALL THE ATHLETES LIVE IS AMAZING. APPARENTLY, THEY HAVE FOUR OF THOSE MACHINES WHERE YOU CAN PUT DIFFERENT FLAVORS IN YOUR SODA.

BURY ME HERE.
OH MY GOD, THIS IS SO GOOD. MAYBE I SHOULDN'T HAVE GIVEN UP ON VOLLEYBALL IN THE EIGHTH GRADE AFTER ALL.
I COULD'VE LIVED IN THIS PARADISE.
BI BKNOW.
SCROLL
SCROLL
HAVE YOU EVER THOUGHT ABOUT GOING VEGAN?
YEAH. IT WOULD BE KIND OF HARD TO DO RIGHT IN THE DORMS, BUT I THINK IT WOULD BE COOL.

IT SEEMS LIKE EVERYONE IS VEGAN. THERE'S THESE PEOPLE THAT MAKE VIDEOS ABOUT EATING ONLY RAW FOODS AND STUFF. IT'S CALLED RAW FRUITARIANISM OR SOMETHING.
THERE'S ONE WOMAN WHO APPARENTLY EATS, LIKE, 30 POUNDS OF FRUIT A WEEK AND DOES COMPETITIVE WEIGHT LIFTING.
SCROLL SCROLL SCROLL

THAT DOESN'T SOUND RIGHT.

MUST NOT BE FOR PEOPLE IN THE MIDWEST. I GUESS IF YOU LIVE IN HAWAII OR AUSTRALIA, YOU COULD DO THAT. YOU WOULD NEVER HAVE TO WORRY ABOUT SCURVY.

WHAT?

NEVER MIND.

IT SOUNDS...RESTRICTIVE. AND EXPENSIVE, AND YOU CAN'T GET ALL YOUR NUTRIENTS AND PROTEIN FROM JUST FRUIT. PLUS, HOW MANY PEOPLE HAVE ACCESS TO THAT MUCH FRESH PRODUCE? EVEN IF YOU LIVE SOMEWHERE TROPICAL.

YEAH...REGULAR VEGANISM IS SUPPOSED TO BE GOOD FOR YOU AND THE ENVIRONMENT, THOUGH, SO I DON'T KNOW. I JUST THINK, LIKE, MAYBE IT WOULD FEEL GOOD TO KNOW I'M DOING SOMETHING POSITIVE WITH MY LIFE.

SURE. I THINK MAYBE YOU SHOULD DO A LITTLE MORE RESEARCH ON THE NUTRITIONAL STUFF, THOUGH.
OTHERWISE, I'M ALL FOR IT.

YEAH, ONCE I BECAME VEGAN, ALL MY ISSUES JUST DISAPPEARED! ISN'T THAT AMAZING?
GASP
WHOA
AH
WOW
SHE HAS NO ISSUES!
POP
DON'T THEY LIVE IN OUR DORM?
SWEET MERCY

TUESDAY MORNING, 8:47 A.M., EARLY OCTOBER.
BUZZ
BUZZ
BUZZ
BUZZ
BUZZ
HEY, WHAT'S UP?
I JUST WOKE UP.
OH, SORRY...IS IT—UH, I...CAN WE TALK?
WHAT'S GOING ON? IS THIS ABOUT THE OTHER NIGHT? SORRY I DRUNK-TEXTED YOU—THAT WAS WEIRD.
NO, NO, THAT'S FINE... I JUST WANTED TO TALK TO YOU ABOUT...US.
WHAT'S UP?
WELL, UM...IT'S HARD TO SAY EXACTLY HOW I FEEL, BUT I JUST CAN'T HELP BUT THINK...I FEEL...THAT IT'S BEEN REALLY HARD DOING THIS LONG-DISTANCE THING, AND I FEEL REALLY BAD, BUT...

I-
AND I DON'T KNOW IF I CAN...
BEN.

I THINK WE SHOULD BREAK UP.

MAYBE WE CAN GET BACK TOGETHER ONCE YOU'RE HOME FOR THE SUMMER-

BUT WE TALKED ABOUT THIS BEFORE I LEFT. I THOUGHT YOU WANTED TO DO THIS.
I KNOW. I JUST...I DON'T THINK I REALLY UNDERSTOOD...I THINK WE SHOULD JUST BE FRIENDS FOR NOW. I REALLY WANT TO STILL BE FRIENDS. I STILL REALLY LIKE YOU.

SARAH?

UM...OK...
SO...

...I'M SORRY. I JUST WASN'T EXPECTING THIS FIRST THING IN THE MORNING. I HAVE CLASS IN, LIKE, AN HOUR...
I KNOW. I'M SORRY.

SNIFF
WELL, I'LL JUST DROP YOUR SWEATSHIRT AND STUFF OFF AT YOUR HOUSE WHEN I'M HOME, I GUESS. YOU STILL HAVE MY DENIM JACKET.
OK.

AND YOU PROMISED MY PARENTS YOU'D WATCH HUEY NEXT WEEKEND WHILE THEY'RE IN ILLINOIS.
I STILL WILL.
OK. WELL.

OK.
SNIFF
SNIFF

I GOTTA GO.
OK. BYE.
WHAT THE HELLLLL!
SOMEONE'S POOPING AND WATCHING NETFLIX IN THE BATHROOM AG—
HEY, WHAT'S GOING ON? ARE YOU OK?
HEH
SNIFF
GUESS WHO'S SINGLE?

Le présent imparfait

LE PRÉSENT IMPARFAIT? OUI.

SOOO, MY BOYFRIEND AND I BROKE UP THIS MORNING.

WHAT? OH NO! CAN I GIVE YOU A HUG?

NOD

I JUST HAVE MY CREATIVE WRITING LECTURE.

DO YOU WANT TO COME OVER AND HAVE SOME ACTUAL DINNER? I HAVE MY CAR ON CAMPUS. I COULD DROP YOU BACK AT YOUR DORM TONIGHT.

REALLY?

DUDE, THAT'S SO NICE.

BUT SERIOUSLY. WHO DUMPS SOMEONE BEFORE NOON?

THE EMOTIONAL PURGE.
DELETE
DELETE
DELETE
DELETE

HEY, SARAH? CAN'T HELP BUT NOTICE YOU'VE BEEN LISTENING TO THE SAME SONG FOR 45 MINUTES. DO YOU WANT TO COME TO THE C-STORE WITH ME?

I THINK I GET WHAT YOU MEANT BY "WE JUST LIVE HERE NOW."

WHAT?

I MISS MY DOG.
YEAH. ME TOO.
WOULD YOU WANNA CUDDLE?
MATTERS
BUR OAK
SPRUCE
SILVER MAPLE
RED PINE
EARTH DAY
CLIMATE STRIKE
2016
TRUTH MATTERS
CHEESE

CRIT GROUP DISCUSSION D
JANE AUSTEN SUPERFAN
SCI-FI EXPERT
RYAN, I LIKED YOUR, UH...COLOR WORDS, BUT YOU COULD PROBABLY BE A LITTLE MORE...SPECIFIC? OTHERWISE, I LIKED THE...RHYTHM AND TEMPO.
OK, SOUNDS GOOD. SARAH, ALL I HAD FOR YOURS WAS THAT IT WAS A LITTLE TOO LONG. YOU CAN DEFINITELY CUT IT DOWN. DID YOU HAVE ANYTHING FOR MINE?
ATHLETE TAKING THIS AS AN ELECTIVE
OH. UH, YEAH. I JUST WROTE MY COMMENTS ON THE SHEET.
LANA DEL REY WANNABE
SORRY, I MAY HAVE GONE A LITTLE OVERBOARD. I LIKE TO BE...SPECIFIC.
SLIDE
ENGLISH DEPARTMENT NEWS
sarahmai
I NEED YOU THERE AS MORAL SUPPORT WHILE I DO LAUNDRY
sarahmai
Personally I'm collecting dirty laundry
103
103
103

HOW WAS YOUR DAY?

IT WAS OK. I MADE EYE CONTACT WITH A DOG EARLIER AND CRIED A LITTLE BIT. YOU?

I HAVE ALL THESE CALC MODULES DUE, AND MY MIDTERM IS IN TWO WEEKS, PLUS ALL THIS PAPERWORK FOR A VOLUNTEER THING I GOT TRAPPED INTO, AND IT'S KILLING ME. ANYWAYS, I'M GOING TO A STUDY GROUP AT THE LIBRARY IN ABOUT 20 MINUTES, IF YOU WANT TO WALK THERE WITH ME. WE COULD GRAB DINNER ON THE WAY BACK.

IN CLASS WE WERE TALKING ABOUT SEPARATING ART FROM THE ARTIST, AND I SAID SOMETHING ABOUT HOW I THINK THAT WE DO IT ALL THE TIME UNKNOWINGLY, THAT A LOT OF THE TIME WE LIKE SOMETHING BEFORE WE KNOW ANYTHING ABOUT THE ARTIST.
OR BEFORE THEY DID WHATEVER BAD THING THEY DID.

LIKE, EVERYONE AGREES IT'S IRRESPONSIBLE TO SEPARATE THE ART FROM THE ARTIST, ESPECIALLY IF THEY'RE ALIVE AND PROFITING STILL. I WAS JUST TRYING TO SAY THAT WE ACCIDENTALLY BREAK THESE RULES ALL THE TIME AND DON'T EVEN REALIZE, SO WHAT'S THE LINE THERE? PLUS, IT'S LIKE WE EACH HAVE OUR OWN MORAL CODES, SO EVERYONE HAS A DIFFERENT IDEA OF WHAT'S REALLY BAD OR JUST KIND OF BAD. A THING MIGHT BE WORTH ENDING A CAREER TO ONE PERSON AND BE FORGIVABLE TO ANOTHER.
I WAS JUST THINKING ABOUT HOW IT'S NOT ALWAYS THAT SIMPLE ONCE YOU KNOW ABOUT THE BAD THING.
OH-KAY...

LIKE, WE ALL KNOW JOHN LENNON SUCKED, SO ARE THE BEATLES ONE-QUARTER BAD? OR IS IT MORE LIKE ONE-HALF BAD BECAUSE HE WROTE A LOT OF THEIR MUSIC? DO WE ALSO IMPLICATE HIS BANDMATES FOR STANDING BY HIM? EVEN THEN, YOU'D HAVE TO ACKNOWLEDGE THE COMPLICATIONS OF THE CROSSOVERS OF THEIR PERSONAL, PROFESSIONAL, AND CREATIVE LIVES, LONG HISTORY AS FRIENDS, PERSONAL TRAUMAS...
I MEAN, I LOVE PAUL MCCARTNEY! HE'S...GOOD, RIGHT?

I REALIZED I BASICALLY SAID, "WAH, WAH, I'M COMPLAINING THAT I CAN'T LISTEN TO CLASSIC ROCK WITHOUT FEELING GUILTY," WHICH SOUNDS SO SELF-CENTERED WHEN THESE THINGS CAUSE ACTUAL HARM TO PEOPLE. AND THEN I REALIZED THAT EVERYONE IN THE ROOM HAD ALREADY TALKED ABOUT THIS BEFORE IN OTHER CLASSES AND I WAS THE ONLY ONE WHO WAS PUTTING IT TOGETHER FOR THE FIRST TIME. I THOUGHT I WAS GOING TO THROW UP.

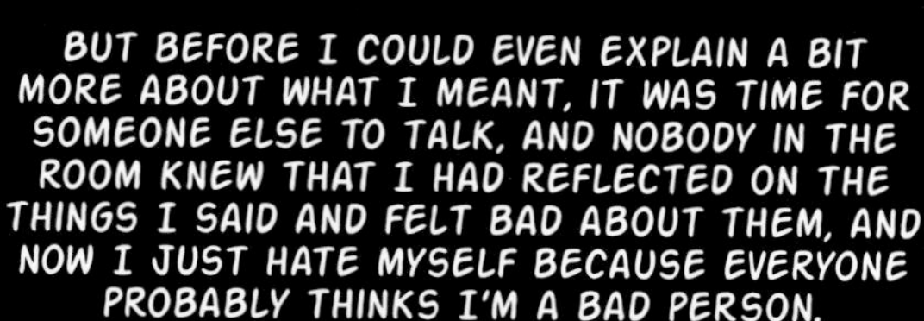

AM I BAD?
UM...NO?
THANKS.
ANYWAY.
NOW I HAVE TO DRAW THIS EGG.

I'M SURE THERE IS A METAPHOR HERE SOMEWHERE.

JAYSEN! I WAS JUST THINKING ABOUT YOU.

OH HEY! WHAT'S UP?

WHAT ARE YOU DOING THIS WEEKEND?

I'M GOING TO A GALLERY OPENING SATURDAY, BUT I'M FREE LATER. WHAT WERE YOU THINKING?

HOW DOES IT LOOK?
UHHH...
JUST THESE, THANKS.
SO WHEN I DID THIS LAST TIME, I KINDA JUST SLATHERED MY WHOLE HEAD IN BLEACH AND WAITED FOR A WHILE.
PLOP!

I'VE DONE WORSE. THIS IS...CHANGE. FOR SURE. I WAS GOING FOR STEVIE, BUT IT'S...
NO, IT'S COOL. IT'S LIKE... DEBBIE HARRY?

OK, WHAT DO WE THINK?
VERY COOL. NOW, THE SHOES...MAY NEED EXPLANATION.

WHAT? I THOUGHT THEY WERE CUTE. THEY'RE CHUNKY.
I THINK THOSE ARE NUN SHOES. BUT...I SEE WHAT YOU'RE GOING FOR. I MEAN, I'M INTO CLOGS, SO I GET IT.

YOU LOOK...DIFFERENT!
I THINK I'M HAVING AN IDENTITY CRISIS.
I CAN SEE THAT.

ANYWAYS, WHAT'S GOING ON WITH YOU? HOW WAS YOUR WEEK?

I GOT A JOB.

WHAT? WHERE? THAT'S GREAT!
AT THE THEATER ON CAMPUS. THEY NEEDED USHERS, SO I APPLIED AND GOT IT. MY FIRST SHIFT IS ON HALLOWEEN! THE TRAVELING BALLET IS DOING *DRACULA.* I'M PUMPED.

THAT'S AWESOME.
WHAT ARE YOU DRINKING?
THAT LOOKS DISGUSTING.

RAW APPLE CIDER VINEGAR AND WATER. IT'S SUPPOSED TO LOWER YOUR BLOOD PRESSURE!
REALLY? IT LOWERS YOUR BLOOD PRESSURE?

ACTUALLY...MAYBE IT'S BLOOD SUGAR. ITS SUPPOSED TO BE GOOD FOR YOUR GUT OR SOMETHING.
YOU SHOULD BE CAREFUL. YOU COULD BURN YOUR ESOPHAGUS.

HOPEFULLY, IF I DRINK THIS EVERY MORNING AND EVENING, I WON'T FEEL THE WEIGHT OF MY RIBS CRUSHING IN ON MY LUNGS AND CAN BREATHE WHEN I GET STRESSED OUT.

...HAVE YOU EVER BEEN TO THERAPY?
...NO?

HALLOWEEN NIGHT ON CAMPUS.
THANKS FOR COMING WITH ME, BY THE WAY. I LIKE SEEING MOVIES BY MYSELF, BUT IF I DON'T HAVE TO, THAT'S EVEN BETTER.
ARE YOU WRITING ABOUT THIS MOVIE FOR THE PAPER?
YEP! IT'S SUPPOSED TO BE PRETTY GOOD.
AS LONG AS THERE ARE NO CLOWNS, I'M SOLD!
AFTER THE MOVIE, WHICH WAS ABOUT CLOWNS.
VARSITY
OPEN
FOR LEASE
SEE, THAT GUY DOESN'T CARE. HE DOESN'T WORRY IF PEOPLE THINK NEGATIVELY ABOUT HIM.
OR HE CARES SO MUCH WHAT PEOPLE THINK OF HIM THAT HE THINKS HE NEEDS TO DRESS UP IN THAT COSTUME AND BE SEEN.
1327

WELL, I FEEL LIKE THAT WOULD ONLY BE THE CASE IF HE WEREN'T WEARING A MASK. LIKE IF HE RAN AROUND IN A SPEEDO EVERY DAY AS HIMSELF INSTEAD OF GOLLUM.
VARSITY
OPEN
FOR LEASE
OPEN
MAYBE HE JUST LIKES THE ATTENTION, EVEN IF IT'S NOT REALLY ABOUT HIM.
TAP
TAP
Are you sure?
Unfollow
Cancel
Unfollow
Unfollow
Unfollow
Un

MIDTERMS. THE EDGE OF BREAKDOWN.

TAP TAP TAP

TAP TAP TAP

PING!

Huey says he misses you very much! Love you, Big Toe

I THINK I'M GETTING SICK.

EVERYONE'S GETTING SICK.

TAP TAP TAP

TAP TAP

TAP TAP TAP TAP

EVERYONE WRITES A PARAGRAPH. IT'S DUE TOMORROW, AND OUR LAST MEMBER HAS WRITTEN ZERO WORDS.
I'M GOING TO KILL HIM.
OR CRY.
I WILL PROBABLY JUST CRY.
YIKES.
UGH! I'VE BEEN TRYING TO WRITE THIS PIECE ABOUT A LOCAL MUSICIAN, BUT SHE KEEPS FLAKING ON OUR INTERVIEW DATES! DO YOU WANT THE PROMOTION OR NOT?
WAIT...OH MY GOD.
WHAT?
I JUST FOUND OUT THAT I GOT INTO THE STUDY-ABROAD PROGRAM OVER WINTER BREAK! I'M GOIN' TO BERLIN!
WHAT? THAT'S SO COOL—I DIDN'T KNOW YOU COULD DO THAT!
I GOTTA CALL MY DAD.
HE'S GONNA BE SO EXCITED!
Google
art school transfer california scholarship
art school transfer california scholarship
scholarships
scholarship federation
art school scholarships canada
art school scholarship uk
TAP TAP TAP TAP TAP T

Miss you, Mom. <3
SM

SO, YOU KNOW HOW I'VE BEEN GOING TO THOSE ECO AND OUTDOORS CLUB MEETINGS EVERY WEEK?
UH...NO, BUT CARRY ON.
THEY'RE HOSTING AN OVERNIGHT CAMPING TRIP AT A STATE PARK JUST OUTSIDE THE CITY THIS WEEKEND.

I KNOW MADDY DOESN'T LIKE ALL THAT CAMPING STUFF, BUT I THOUGHT YOU MIGHT BE INTERESTED IF YOU DON'T HAVE SOMETHING ELSE GOING ON.

I DON'T THINK I HAVE ANYTHING IMPORTANT HAPPENING THIS WEEKEND.

WHO AM I KIDDING? I DEFINITELY DON'T HAVE ANYTHING IMPORTANT HAPPENING THIS WEEKEND.

IT'LL BE COLD, BUT THEY PROVIDE THE TENTS AND ALL THE FOOD AND FIREWOOD AND STUFF. SO WE JUST SHOW UP! I THINK YOU MIGHT LIKE THE PEOPLE. IT'LL BE FUN!

LOTS OF FUN.

HEY, CLARK.

WHAT IS *UP*, MY NEW FRIENDS? HAVING FUN? ROASTED A TOFU WEENIE?

UNCE
UNCE
UNCE
UNCE

YEH-HESSS, HACK THAT SACK OVER HERE, MY GUY!

RUSTLE
RUSTLE
RUSTLE
IS THAT A SQUIRREL?
NO, I THINK IT'S THE TENT NEXT TO US.

IS THAT GOOD?
UH-HUH, YEAH.
WHAT IF I-

THEY'RE HAVING SEX!
WHAT?

RUSTLE
RUSTLE
RUSTLE
RUSTLE
UHHH-

OH MY GOD!

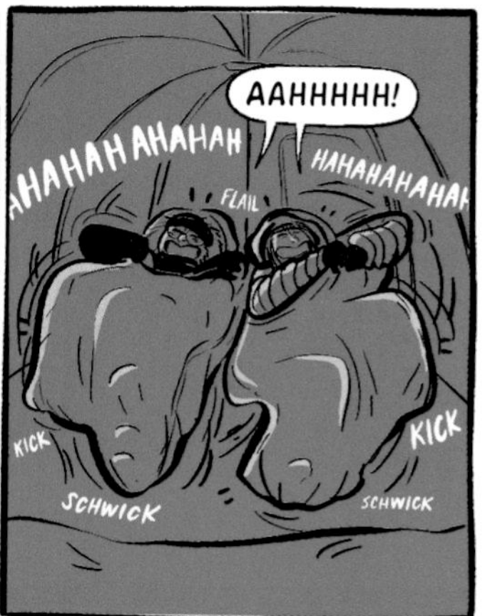
AAHHHHH!
AHAHAHAHAHAH
HAHAHAHAHAH
FLAIL
KICK
KICK
SCHWICK
SCHWICK

I THINK MY TEARS ARE FROZEN.
MINE TOO.
OH, MAN. WHOO! HOO-HOO...

HA
HA

RUSTLE
RUSTLE
RUSTLE
RUSTLE
RUSTLE

SARAH?
YEAH?

HAVE YOU...
DONE IT?

UM...
...YEAH. YOU?
UH...
...NO, NOT...NO.

DON'T WORRY—IT'S NOT THAT BIG OF A DEAL.
I KNOW.

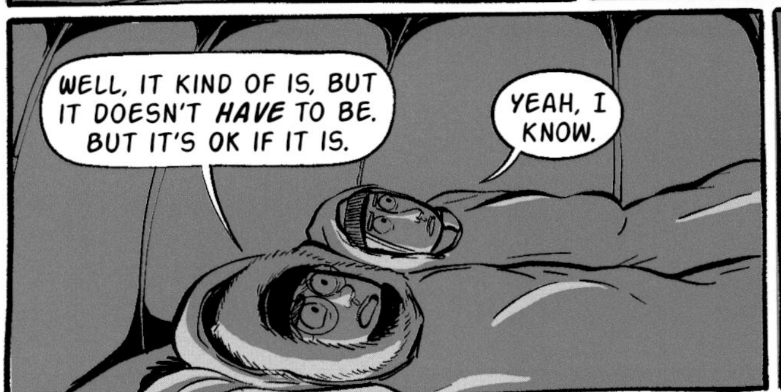
WELL, IT KIND OF IS, BUT IT DOESN'T HAVE TO BE. BUT IT'S OK IF IT IS.
YEAH, I KNOW.

RUSTLE
RUSTLE
RUSTLE

EVERYONE ACTS SO CASUAL ABOUT IT. SOMEHOW EVERYBODY KNOWS EXACTLY WHAT TO DO, LIKE IT'S COMMON SENSE, BUT I JUST—WELL, I DON'T SEEM TO QUITE...
I DON'T KNOW. IT CAN BE FUN, THOUGH, DON'T GET ME WRONG. IT'LL HAPPEN WHEN IT'S MEANT TO.
EH, I DON'T KNOW.

I HAVEN'T KISSED ANYONE YET.
OH.

RUSTLE RUSTLE RUSTLE RUSTLE RUSTLE
I BET CLARK WOULD KISS YOU IF YOU ASKED NICELY. HE'S VERY ACCOMMODATING.
HA HA.
NO THANKS.
I WAS JUST KIDDING.
SORRY.
DO YOU THINK THEY KNOW WE CAN HEAR THEM?
I DON'T KNOW. MAYBE WE SHOULD THROW A PEBBLE AT THEIR TENT.
THEY'RE SO LOUD IT MIGHT NEED TO BE A BOULDER.
SHHHHHHHHHH!
HEHEHEHEHEHE.

END OF NOVEMBER. CRUNCH TIME.
IT CAN'T BE THANKSGIVING ALREADY. I HAVE **SO MUCH** TO DO.
I STILL NEED TO FIGURE OUT HOW I'M GETTING HOME. DID YOU GUYS DO THAT ALREADY?
I BOUGHT MY TICKETS A COUPLE OF WEEKS AGO. THE BUSES MIGHT BE FULL BY NOW.
ACTUAL LAST TICKET

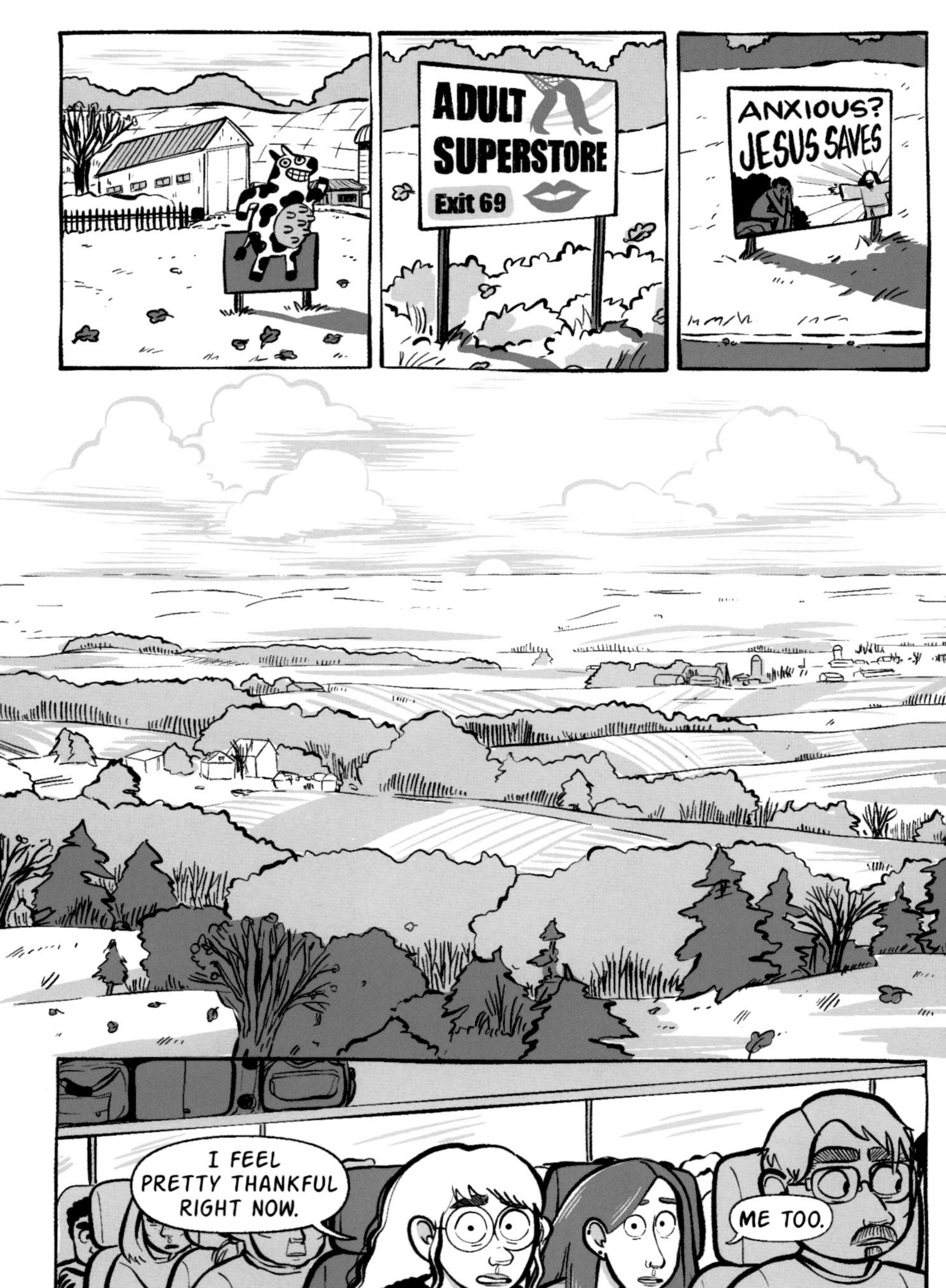
ADULT
SUPERSTORE
Exit 69
ANXIOUS?
JESUS SAVES
I FEEL PRETTY THANKFUL RIGHT NOW.
ME TOO.

SARAH'S HOME!
HAS THIS HOUSE ALWAYS SMELLED LIKE THIS?

BUZZ
BUZZ
BUZZ
YELLO?
ARE YOU HOME YET?
YEAH, I JUST GOT BACK!

SQUEEE!

HOP
HOP
HOP
EHEHEHE
EHEHE

AGHH! I HAVE SO MUCH TO TELL YOU.
YOU LOOK GREAT, BY THE WAY. VERY STEVIE.
OH, THANKS, I–

I CAN'T WAIT ANY LONGER: I'M MOVING TO NEW YORK!
THIS SUMMER!

OH! I THOUGHT YOU WERE GOING IN THE FALL.
THAT'S...
SOONER.

I APPLIED TO A MUSIC PROGRAM, AND THEY ARE LETTING ME START OVER THE SUMMER! THEY LIKED THE SAMPLES I'VE BEEN WORKING ON, THE ONES I WROTE LAST YEAR, REMEMBER?
I'M LIVING WITH VINNY.
THAT'S...
THAT'S SO GREAT!
SNIP
SNIP
SNIP

THANKSGIVING. ILLINOIS. KIDS' TABLE.
PICK PICK PICK
SO, WHAT KINDS OF THINGS ARE YOU INTO NOW? DO YOU LIKE...SCIENCE?
WHY IS IT SO HARD TO TALK TO YOU?
YEAH. I LIKE SCIENCE.
SARAH, HOW'S SCHOOL GOING?
ARE YOU STILL DATING THAT NICE BOY WE MET OVER THE SUMMER?
UH, NO, WE BROKE UP. SCHOOL IS GOOD.
THAT'S TOO BAD-HE WAS SO NICE!
CHOMP

COME ON! NOT ANOTHER ONE!
ZZZZZ

ANNUAL THANKSGIVING ALLERGY ATTACK.

ACHOO! ACHOO! ACHOO!
ACHOO! ACHOO! ACHOO!

THE VIZSLA?
YEP.

MOM JUST GOT HER STEROID SHOT.
IF SHE SEES YOU, SHE'LL ACTUALLY KILL YOU.
FLICK FLICK

CRUNCH

SCOOT SCOOT

HOLIDAYS HAVEN'T BEEN THE SAME WITHOUT GRANDMA.

EXIT

FRIDAY, 4:30 P.M.
THERAPY POOL.

I'VE FELT THIS WAY AT HOME, TOO, BUT IT'S WORSE AT SCHOOL. I HAVE FUN SOMETIMES, BUT I MOSTLY HAVE THIS FEELING...I DUNNO.

WHAT'S GOING ON? IS IT BEN? DO YOU NOT LIKE THE CAMPUS? YOU COULD TRANSFER HOME LIKE ROB DID.

UGHHH, NO, JUST...I WAS FEELING WEIRDLY OPTIMISTIC, AND NOW EVERYTHING'S FALLING APART AT THE SEAMS AGAIN. AND IT'S NOT THE BREAKUP OR SCHOOL, IT'S JUST...

LAST YEAR I WAS IN PLAYS AND DID CHOIR AND HUNG OUT AND PEOPLE SAID HI TO ME, AND NOW I JUST WORRY ALL THE TIME AND WRITE PAPERS AND DRAW.

I DON'T KNOW. PROBABLY. I MEAN, I WANT TO. I TRY TO. I MEET PEOPLE ALL THE TIME. I JUST THINK SOMETHING IS WRONG WITH ME. EVERYONE ELSE IS ***DOING*** THINGS. I ***USED*** TO DO THINGS.
I USED TO KNOW HOW TO JUST BE, BUT NOW I WORRY ABOUT EVERYTHING AND GET STUCK.
WELL, I FELT THE SAME WAY AT YOUR AGE. EVERYONE WAS ALWAYS GETTING JOBS AND DATING AND GOING TO PARTIES, AND I HAD MY ARTWORK. I WAS ALONE. BUT I FIGURED IT OUT. YOU CAN'T GET DISTRACTED BY THIS STUFF. SCHOOL IS THE MOST IMPORTANT THING.
SPLASH SPLASH
HEY, THIS WILL ALL GO INTO A SCREENPLAY SOMEDAY. YOU CAN WRITE ABOUT ME.
NOOOO, I JUST WANT TO BE A LITTLE BABY AGAIN. RETURN ME TO THE WOMB.
SPLISH

PAH
WAS I WEARING EYELINER?
AAAGHHHHHHHHH!
RUB RUB
HOW'S THAT?

SATURDAY, 8:00 P.M.
I NEEDED TO GET OUT OF THE HOUSE. MY FAMILY IS DRIVING ME NUTS. THANKS FOR INVITING ME, BY THE WAY.
WELL, YEAH, WHY WOULD WE NOT INVITE YOU?
OH, I DON'T KNOW—I THOUGHT YOU ALL MIGHT FEEL WEIRD BECAUSE YOU GUYS HANG OUT WITH BEN, AND IF WE BOTH WERE THERE, IT MIGHT BE AWKWARD OR WHATEVER.
OH. NO, DUDE, HE'S NOT EVEN GONNA BE THERE. HE'S DOING SOMETHING WITH HIS FRIENDS WHO ARE IN TOWN FROM MADISON. PLUS, WE'RE ALL ADULTS—WE COULD HANDLE IT.
YEAH...

AH! I MISSED YOU SO MUCH!

COME! WE'RE ALL JUST IN THE LIVING ROOM.

HI.
HEY.
SUP?

HEY, AMELIE, HOW'S IT GOING?
OH MY GOSH, IT'S SO GREAT TO SEE YOU! HOW'S MINNESOTA? I WANT TO HEAR ALL ABOUT IT!

IT'S...GOOD, YEAH. LEARNING STUFF, ALL THAT. HOW'S MADISON?
I LOVE IT! IT'S BEEN SO GOOD—I JOINED THIS REALLY FANTASTIC WOMEN'S ORGANIZATION AND AM LOVING MY CLASSES.
AND, Y'KNOW, HAVING SOME FUN.

THAT'S AWESOME! I'M GLAD YOU'RE LIKING IT.

WELL, NOW THAT WE'RE ALL HERE...

CLINK
CLINK
GUESS I'M SLEEPING OVER TONIGHT.

11:00 P.M.

DING DONG!
OH, HEY! YOU CAME! WE DIDN'T THINK YOU WERE GONNA MAKE IT.
YEAH, MAN, I WOULDN'T MISS IT.

NO.

I COULD JUMP THROUGH THE WINDOW AND THEN RUN OUTSIDE AND CALL MY MOM TO PICK ME UP.

BUT IT'S TOO LATE.

MAYBE I COULD JUST STAY IN HERE FOR A WHILE AND THEN SNEAK OUT AND WALK.

NO. IF I STAY IN HERE TOO LONG, THEY'RE GOING TO THINK I WAS POOPING.

POOPING FOR A LONG TIME. I NEED TO GET OUT OF HERE RIGHT NOW.

OH, OK.
POP OFF.
CHIPS
DO I LOOK OK?
YEAH, OF COURSE, YOU LOOK GREAT. WHY?

I WASN'T EXPECTING *SOMEBODY* TO BE HERE, SO I DIDN'T REALLY DRESS APPROPRIATELY.

OH YEAH. SORRY, ZEKE INVITED HIM. WE ALL THOUGHT IT WOULD BE OK SINCE BEN TOLD US YOU GUYS ARE STILL FRIENDS AND TEXT AND STUFF.

I MEAN, WE'VE TEXTED A COUPLE OF TIMES ABOUT, LIKE, NOTHING.
YOU KNOW WHAT, IT'S FINE. I'M FINE.
I AM GROWN UP AND CAN HANDLE THIS.

GLUG
GLUG
GLUG
GULP
GULP
GULP
OH.
I SEE.

HEEYYY.
YOU'RE BACK! WE THOUGHT YOU RAN AWAY.
SCOOT
HA HA. NOT THIS TIME.
HEY.
NOPE. NOPE.
HEY... I'M ACTUALLY, UH, GONNA HELP EMMA WITH THE SNACKS. UM...BYE.

3:00 A.M.
I NEED TO SLEEP. I'M TAKING THE TRAIN BACK TO SCHOOL TOMORROW MORNING.

YOU CAN SLEEP WITH ME IN MY BED.
CAN WE CUDDLE?

6:00 A.M.

ZZZZ

FINN, WE GOTTA GO.
HUH?
SHHH. FINN, YOU HAVE TO TAKE ME HOME.
BYE, EMMA. LOVE YOU. I'LL CALL YOU LATER.
MM-HMM.
PECK

CLICK

LIZ?
YOU WILL NOT BELIEVE THE DAY I JUST HAD.

YOU'RE BACK SO LATE.
SOMEONE *DIED* ON THE BUS.
THEY HAD TO STOP AND WAIT FOR AN AMBULANCE TO ARRIVE, AND WE ALL SAT IN OUR SEATS UNTIL THEY CAME AND GOT HIM OFF THE BUS.

WHAT?
I DON'T WANT TO TALK ABOUT IT.
DID YOU EAT DINNER?

I WAS GONNA HEAD OVER AND JOIN MADDY FOR NUG NIGHT.
I NEED NUG NIGHT.

LANA LEFT HER GOLDFISH HERE OVER BREAK, AND IT DIED. SHE HASN'T THROWN IT OUT, AND NOW SHE'S AT HER BOYFRIEND'S APARTMENT.
NUG NIGHT
THAT'S GOTTA SMELL, RIGHT?
DEATH LINGERS IN 202 FRONTIER HALL.
CHEW
IT DIDN'T DESERVE THIS.
LORDE
WHAT DO WE DO?
I DON'T KNOW.
IT'S NOT MY FISH.

WELL, WE HAVE TO DO SOMETHING.
I'M NOT TOUCHING IT.
I'VE HAD ENOUGH OF DEATH TODAY.
MCTITTY NEEDS TO CROSS OVER TO THE AFTERLIFE.
SHE NAMED IT MCTITTY?
YEP.
SIGH
HOW DO WE DO THIS?
HAVE EITHER OF YOU EVER BEEN TO A FUNERAL?
YEAH.
FIVE.
OH.
SORRY.

REST IN PEACE, MCTITTY.

WHOOOSHHH

WHOSE ARE THOSE?
LANA'S.
GOLDFISH
BAKED CRACKERS
CHEESE

SHE WOULDN'T NOTICE IF I HAD, LIKE, A HANDFUL, RIGHT?

WHO CARES. I'M STILL MAD ABOUT MCTITTY.

GOLDFISH AREN'T VEGAN.

WHATEVER.

JANGLE
JANGLE

CLICK

QUICK, PUT THEM BACK!
GOLDFISH
CHEESE

OH, HEY, LANA. WHAT'S UP?

HI.
I'M JUST STOPPING BY TO GET MY STUFF FOR TOMORROW.

THIS IS LIZ AND SARAH, BY THE WAY.

I KNOW YOU WERE EATING MY GOLDFISH.

IT WAS...FINE. I HAD THE PLEASURE OF SEEING BEN OVER BREAK.
OH, NICE!
I GOT TO SERVE WARM BEER TO MIDDLE-AGED DADS.
THEN I CAME BACK HERE AND APPLIED FOR APPRENTICESHIPS. OVERALL, NOT BAD!
I 'OPE YOU TWO AHR' TALKING ABOUT *LE PASSÉ IMPARFAIT!*
I BETTER GET THE SNOW TIRES ON.

THAT NIGHT.

DING!

WHAT?

WHAT?

ACCOUNT NOTICE

Your spring course enrollment slot occurred on 11/23. Please contact an adviser for further assistance with registration.

YOU HAD TO CHECK YOUR STUDENT ACCOUNT FOR IT. YOU CLICK THE ACADEMICS TAB AND THEN AGAIN UNDER THE REGISTRATION SUB BOX.

CLICK THE HIGHLIGHTED THING WITH THE SHOPPING CART.

I RAN INTO MY EX THIS WEEKEND, AND I WAS WEARING *CROCS.* FLING ME INTO THE SUN!
SARAH?
HI, I'M KIRSTEN, YOUR NEW ADVISER!
OH, I THOUGHT I WAS MEETING WITH CARI.
I HAD HER FOR THE FIRST MEETING.
OH, YEAH, NO. I'M YOUR ADVISER. CARI WAS JUST FOR WELCOME WEEK.
THIS WAY.
OH-KAY, SO I SEE YOU CAME IN TO REGISTER!
UH, YES. I MISSED MY SLOT BY A COUPLE OF DAYS. I DIDN'T REALIZE IT HAD ALREADY PASSED.

MM-HMM, I SEE THAT. SO YOU'RE THINKING OF ENGLISH AS YOUR MAJOR. OH-KAY...AND MAYBE ART?
ALL RIGHT...NOW, A LOT OF THE ENGLISH COURSES FOR FRESHMEN ARE PRETTY MUCH FILLED UP...BUT I SEE YOU CAME IN WITH A COUPLE OF A.P. CREDITS...HMMM...
I WAS THINKING I COULD START ON SOME HIGHER-LEVEL ENGLISH COURSES FOR THE NEXT SEMESTER. SOME OF THE DEGREE REQUIREMENTS, IF POSSIBLE.
CLACK CLACK CLACK
MMM, OH-KAY. SO LET ME SHOW YOU THE REQUIREMENTS FOR GRADUATION, PRINTED OUT HERE...
THUD
...AND HERE ARE YOUR REQUIREMENTS FOR THE ENGLISH MAJOR. REMEMBER THAT YOU CAN EITHER CHOOSE THE ENGLISH ***WRITING*** TRACK OR THE ENGLISH ***LITERATURE*** TRACK.
THOSE ARE ***DIFFERENT?***
CLACK CLACK CLACK
CLICK
THUD
AND HERE ARE YOUR OPTIONS FOR COURSES THIS SEMESTER.

Jaysen

Which French class are you in next semester?

SM

LATER THAT WEEK.
REMEMBER, THE FINAL PROJECTS ARE DUE ON THE LAST DAY OF LECTURE. PLEASE EMAIL ME IF YOU HAVE ANY PROBLEMS SO YOU DON'T SLIP THROUGH THE CRACKS IN OUR BUREAUCRACY.
HEY, SARAH, CAN I TALK TO YOU FOR A MINUTE?
UH, SURE, IS EVERYTHING OK?
OH YES. NO LITERARY DISASTERS. I JUST WANTED TO ASK YOU—THE FINAL COURSE LECTURE IS COMING UP, AND WE ALWAYS HAVE A STUDENT FROM EACH DISCUSSION SECTION READ SOME OF THEIR WORK. I WAS WONDERING IF YOU WANTED TO SHARE ONE OF YOUR PIECES.
OH! UH, YEAH, I CAN DO THAT!
I CAN DO THAT.

LATER.
JE SERAI, TU SERAS, IL/ELLE SERA...
I'VE BEEN THINKING ABOUT TRANSFERRING TO AN ART SCHOOL.
OH YEAH? ANY AROUND HERE?
NO, MOST OF THEM ARE IN CALIFORNIA.
OH.
I'M SCARED I'M WASTING MY TIME HERE, BUT I'M ALSO SCARED THAT ART SCHOOL MIGHT BE A HUGE MISTAKE.
WELL, MAYBE YOU JUST NEED TO MEET MORE PEOPLE LIKE YOU. ACTUALLY, I'M GOING TO A HOLIDAY PARTY NEXT WEEKEND, AND A LOT OF US FROM THE B.F.A. PROGRAM ARE GOING TO BE THERE. DO YOU WANT TO COME?
OUI, JE VOUDRAIS Y ALLER.
I AM TOTALLY GONNA FAIL THIS CLASS. IS IT TOO LATE TO SEDUCE THE PROFESSOR?

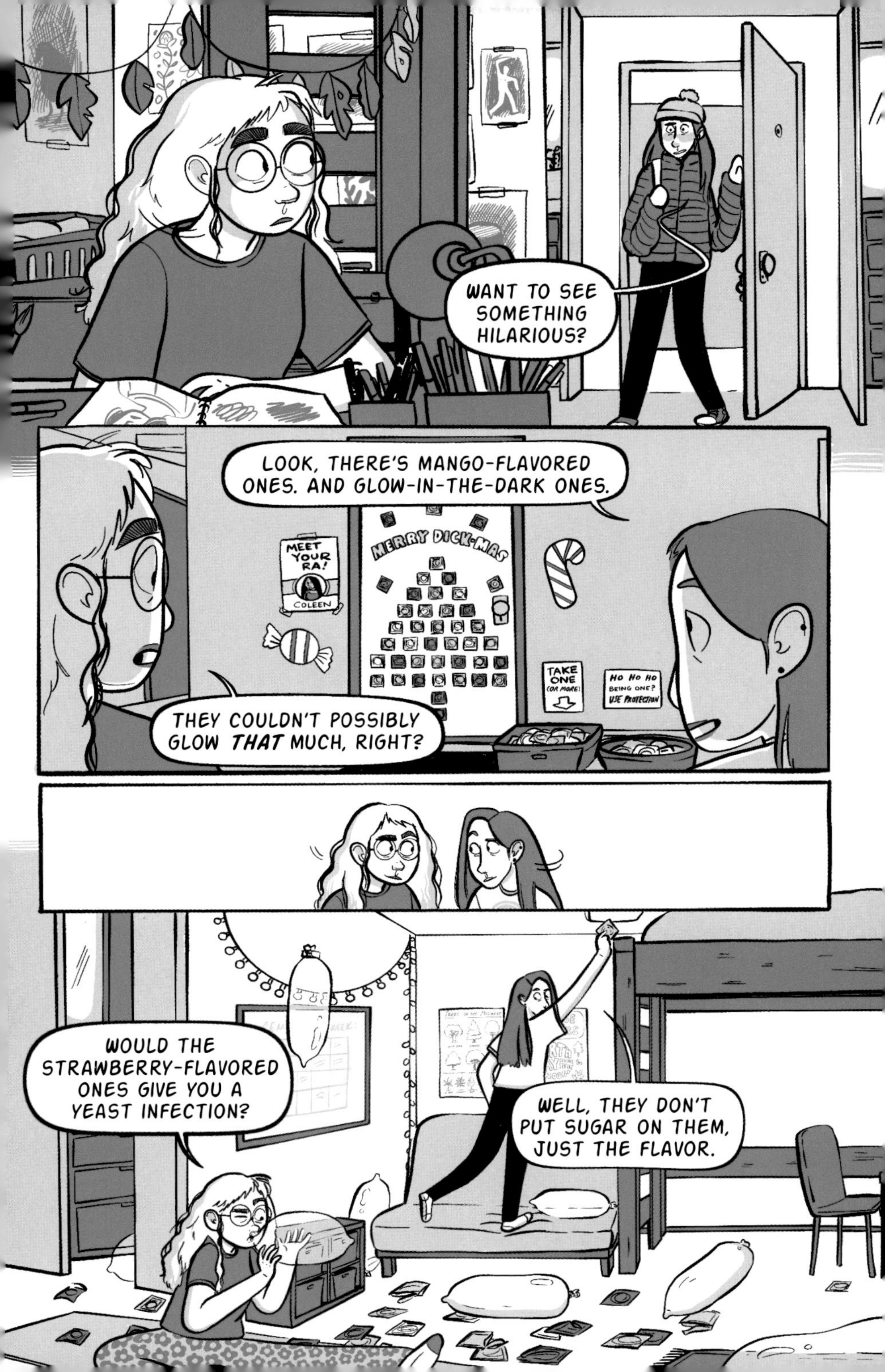

WANT TO SEE SOMETHING HILARIOUS?
LOOK, THERE'S MANGO-FLAVORED ONES. AND GLOW-IN-THE-DARK ONES.
MEET YOUR RA!
COLEEN
MERRY DICK-MAS
TAKE ONE (OR MORE)
HO HO HO BEING ONE? USE PROTECTION
THEY COULDN'T POSSIBLY GLOW *THAT* MUCH, RIGHT?
WOULD THE STRAWBERRY-FLAVORED ONES GIVE YOU A YEAST INFECTION?
WELL, THEY DON'T PUT SUGAR ON THEM, JUST THE FLAVOR.

I WONDER WHAT IT TASTES LIKE, THOUGH.

STRAWBERRY.

BUT, LIKE, DOES IT ALSO TASTE LIKE RUBBER? OR PLASTIC? LIKE WHEN YOU LEAVE WATER IN A PLASTIC CUP TOO LONG AND IT TASTES BAD.

THERE'S ONLY ONE WAY TO FIND OUT.

YEAH, IT TASTES LIKE STRAWBERRY PLASTIC.

OK, QUICK, TURN OFF THE LIGHTS!

FLIP

FINALS APPROACHETH.
I DON'T KNOW WHY I THOUGHT IT WOULD BE INTERESTING TO WRITE ABOUT FEMINIST LITERATURE THROUGH A FREUDIAN LENS, BUT IT'S NOT REALLY WORKING. THIS PROJECT SUCKS.
ODD CHOICE.
"HER MOUTH WAS A FOUNTAIN OF DELIGHT." IT FEELS DIRTY TO EVEN QUOTE THAT. GROSS. MATT'S GONNA READ THIS. SHOULD'VE THOUGHT ABOUT THAT EARLIER.
WHERE'S LIZ? I THOUGHT SHE'S USUALLY BACK BY EIGHT ON TUESDAYS.
SHE'S AT SOME NEW CLUB MEETING TONIGHT AT THE UNION. THE SOIL CLUB, I THINK.
SOIL? LIKE DIRT?
YEAH, I DON'T KNOW. SHE SAID SOMETHING ABOUT WANTING TO MEET NEW PEOPLE, THEN LEFT.
SHE SEEMED KINDA IRRITATED.
ARE YOU GUYS STILL UP FOR THAT MOVIE PREMIERE NEXT WEEK?
CRAP. I TOTALLY FORGOT. I JUST TOLD A FRIEND I'D GO TO A HOLIDAY PARTY WITH HIM THAT NIGHT.
OH...IT'S OK. I'LL JUST ASK MY COWORKER IF HE WANTS TO COME.
I'M SORRY. I CAN'T BELIEVE I DIDN'T REMEMBER THAT.
IT'S FINE.

ACTUALLY, I SHOULD PROBABLY GO. I HAVE TO PREPARE FOR MY AUDITION TOMORROW.
I'LL SEE YOU LATER.

WHAT THE HELL?
When they don't have your
favorite flavor of kombucha lol
Save
TAP

143♥

Ahaha love

Lol!

HOLIDAY ART PARTY.
YOU LOOK GREAT! IS YOUR HAIR DIFFERENT?
YEAH, I TRIMMED IT A LITTLE. I'M NOT OVERDRESSED, AM I? IS THE LIPSTICK TOO MUCH?
I THINK OTHER PEOPLE WILL BE WEARING LIPSTICK– DON'T WORRY.
MY RIBS HURT.
GAH. I CAN'T BREATHE.
IT'S GONNA BE FUN! EXHALE.
HEY! JAYSEN! FRIENDS! COME ON IN. WE'RE ALL IN THE LIVING ROOM.

WELL, I JUST THINK HER WORK IS A LITTLE DERIVATIVE. A GOLD CAR? REALLY?
SHE SAID IT DOESN'T MATTER WHAT HER INTENTION WAS WITH THE PIECE. I FEEL LIKE SHE WAS JUST SAYING THAT BECAUSE SHE WANTED AN EXCUSE TO MAKE SOMETHING EXPENSIVE FOR NO REASON.
WELL, I MEAN, SHE'S NOT WRONG. I DON'T REALLY CARE. GET THAT UNIVERSITY COIN AND MAKE WHATEVER YOU WANT.
MEW
ORGANIC EGG NOG
SNIP SNIP SNIP
YEAH, I'M A G.W.S.S. MAJOR.
OH. COOL!
WHAT THE HELL IS A GEE WHIZ?
HOW ABOUT YOU?
I'M NOT SURE YET. MAYBE ENGLISH.
I HAVE SOME TIME BEFORE I NEED TO DECIDE.

WAIT—ARE YOU A *FRESHMAN?*
UNFORTUNATELY.
OH, I THOUGHT YOU WERE A JUNIOR!
THAT'S WHAT I SAID!
DO YOU KNOW WHAT YOU WANT TO DO WITH ENGLISH?
UM, I WANT TO DO ILLUSTRATION, ACTUALLY.
BOOKS, MAGAZINES, THAT KIND OF STUFF.
OH...
COMMERCIAL ART.
COOL.
CAPITALIST PIG!

CHEERS.

CHEERS.

CHEERS.

SIGH
TO DO
THE AWAKENING
KATE CHOPIN
Yoga poses for stressed out losers
Yoga poses for stressed out losers
Yoga poses for stressed out losers

FINALS WEEK ARRIVETH.
sob
EXAMEN FINAL
SARAH MAI
NOW I WILL READ THE ENTIRE *BEE MOVIE* SCRIPT. JUST KIDDING. UH...

LAST DAY :)
HAVE A NICE BREAK!
Sarah Mai
Creative Writing 05
Final
Classroom Prayers
The leaves outside pane-glass window
Shake like my knees with anticipation
Of colder things to come.
I scribble a few notes down
And bite a hangnail
The small sliver of the moon
Falls on my paper
I brush it away.
No wonder we fall asleep again
The moon is still in the sky
While we sip our coffees.
Morning class, poison in the ear
Dripped slowly in, a cold brew
No more pen, no more paper
We dream of pillows and blankets
I sit and dream awake
Watching the leaves shiver and sleep
And feel a silent prayer built in me
That the lights will shiver and sleep too.
HAPPY
Sarah Mai
Group 10
Freud and Feminist Fantesies
Final Paper
Textual Analysis

I'M COMING BACK TO CAMPUS RIGHT AFTER CHRISTMAS TO WORK. I DON'T HAVE A BEDROOM AT HOME ANYMORE SINCE MY SISTER DECIDED SHE NEEDS HER OWN SPACE.
OH. YOU COULD COME STAY WITH ME!
NO, NO, IT'S COOL. THEY PAY TIME AND A HALF DURING BREAK. THE TEXTBOOK PRICES FOR NEXT SEMESTER ARE OUT OF CONTROL, SO IT'LL BE WORTH IT.
I'M COMING BACK, TOO. THE CLASS TRIP HAS TO FLY TO BERLIN TOGETHER–
SO I'M ONLY HOME UNTIL THE END OF HANUKKAH.
OH, BEFORE I FORGET–
MY MOM SENT THESE FOR YOU GUYS.
I GOT MONKEY PAJAMAS.
I WAS WONDERING WHERE THOSE CAME FROM.

JUST CALL MY DAD STEVE, OR HE'LL MAKE THE "THAT'S MY FATHER'S NAME" JOKE.
DON'T WORRY. PARENTS LOVE ME.
THANK YOU SO MUCH FOR THE RIDE, MR. FELDSTEIN! UH, STEVE.
NO PROBLEM! HOP IN. YOU'VE MET JACK.
THIS IS MY PARTNER, FRANK.
SLAM
HE DID NOT DO THAT. YOU'RE SERIOUS?
I'M NOT KIDDING—MR. SCHNEIDER LITERALLY DID. THEY ALMOST FIRED HIM!

CHRISTMAS EVE.
NOW, IF YOU DON'T LIKE IT, I HAVE ALL THE GIFT RECEIPTS SO WE CAN TAKE IT BACK NEXT WEEK.

FAMILY TIME.
I JUST DON'T UNDERSTAND WHY THEY SHOW PEOPLE PEEING ON TV SO MUCH NOW.
MOM, IT'S CALLED REALISM. IT'S GRITTY.
8:45

OBLIGATORY CHRISTMAS MASS.
INRI
HAPPY BIRTHDAY.
ON THIS DAY, WE ARE REMINDED THAT GOD COMES TO US IN MOMENTS OF DARKNESS. LET YOUR HEARTS BE FILLED WITH HIS UNWAVERING LOVE.

CHRISTMAS NIGHT.
CHRISTMAS TO NEW YEAR'S PURGATORY.
I'M SO GLAD WE CAME TO THIS COFFEE SHOP TO SIT TOGETHER AND AVOID EYE CONTACT WITH EVERYONE.
12:01 A.M., A NEW YEAR.

LIFEGUARD CERTIFICATION COURSE, DAY ONE.
PLEASE DON'T TOUCH MY BOOB.
PLEASE DON'T TOUCH MY BOOB.
SHIVER
TWO WEEKS LATER.
CERTIFIED.
AMERICAN RED CROSS
Certificate of Completion
SARAH MAI
3FT

HI, SEÑORA BARTLEY.
FAMILY DUTIES.

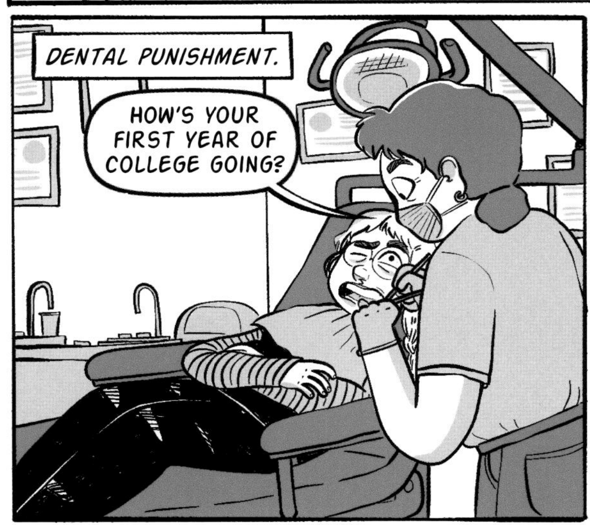
DENTAL PUNISHMENT.
HOW'S YOUR FIRST YEAR OF COLLEGE GOING?

PICK
PICK

MORE FAMILY BONDING.
8:45

NOW THE BAKERS MUST DO **LITERALLY EVERYTHING** PERFECTLY OR EVERYONE WILL DIE!

WHAT ARE YOU WATCHING?

NOTHING. BAKING STUFF.

THE CUSTARD FLAVOR OF THE DAY IS TIRAMISU IF YOU WANT TO GO GET SOME.
I KNOW YOU LIKE THAT ONE.

I'M TRYING TO BE VEGAN. IF I EAT THAT, IT'LL RUIN MY WHOLE WEEK.

SO...

DO YOU LIKE BEING HOME?

I DON'T KNOW. IT'S FINE.

YOU SEEM KIND OF UPSET.

I'M NOT. IT'S FINE.

ARE YOU SAD BECAUSE BEN'S HERE?
NO, WHY WOULD I BE UPSET ABOUT THAT?
BECAUSE HE DUMPED YOU.
...WE BROKE UP MUTUALLY.
MOM SAID HE BROKE UP WITH YOU.
IT WAS MUTUAL. HE JUST SAID IT FIRST. ALSO, I'M NOT SAD ABOUT IT ANYMORE.
OK.
DO YOU WANT SOME OF THIS?
GURGLE
GURGLE
UGGHHH

BACK TO REAL LIFE.
I KNOW I ALREADY SAID THIS, BUT I REALLY THINK YOU SHOULD TAKE SOME BUSINESS CLASSES WHILE YOU'RE AT SCHOOL. I'VE ALWAYS SEEN YOU AS A C.E.O.—YOU'RE SO ARTICULATE. YOU COULD DO REALLY WELL.
10 YOGA POSES FOR SORE NECK
I ALREADY TOLD YOU, YOU CAN'T TAKE THOSE CLASSES IF YOU'RE NOT ENROLLED IN THE BUSINESS SCHOOL. THEY'RE OBSESSED WITH BEING EXCLUSIVE OR WHATEVER. ALSO, BEING A C.E.O. SOUNDS TERRIBLE, DAD. I'D PROBABLY GIVE MYSELF ULCERS.
YOU NEED TO CONTROL THE STRESS. YOU'VE HIT A WALL.
FUTURE C.E.O.!!
WELL, MAYBE OVER THE SUMMER YOU CAN AUDIT SOME CLASSES AT THE COMMUNITY COLLEGE WITH YOUR BROTHER.
SPEND SOME TIME TOGETHER DEVELOPING LIFE SKILLS.

My Life
Billy Joel
WHAT? YOU DON'T LIKE BILLY JOEL? EVERYONE LIKES BILLY JOEL.
UH-UH. NOT THIS ONE.
MY FRIEND THIERRY FROM HIGH SCHOOL PLAYED THIS ALBUM EVERY SINGLE DAY FOR MONTHS AFTER HE GOT IT OUR JUNIOR YEAR. IT'S GOOD, BUT I CAN'T LISTEN TO IT ANYMORE. EVEN AFTER SO MUCH TIME.
FINN DID THAT WITH SUFJAN LAST YEAR.
I WONDER HOW HE'S DOING...I HAVEN'T TALKED TO HIM IN A COUPLE OF YEARS. LAST TIME WE SPOKE, HE WAS GETTING DIVORCED AND MOVING TO NASHVILLE.
DON'T YOU HAVE HIS PHONE NUMBER? YOU SHOULD JUST CALL HIM.
I HAVE. WE KEEP MISSING EACH OTHER'S CALLS. LIFE GETS IN THE WAY. YOU FORGET. TIME STARTS MOVING FASTER AFTER HIGH SCHOOL.

BERLIN ITSELF WAS AMAZING, BUT THERE WAS WAAAY MORE CLASS STUFF THAN ANY OF US ANTICIPATED.

ALSO, I THINK A LOT OF THE GROUP ALREADY KNEW ONE ANOTHER, SO IT WAS KIND OF CLIQUEY. LIKE HIGH SCHOOL.

THAT'S TOO BAD.

IT WAS COOL, THOUGH. IT WAS GOOD TO GET SOME EXTRA CREDITS DURING BREAK. MY WHOLE LIFE IS ABOUT TO BE TAKEN OVER BY REHEARSALS. PLUS, THEY'RE LOOKING FOR A NEW EDITOR AT THE PAPER, SO I HAVE TO REALLY PERFORM THIS SEMESTER.

FIRST DAY OF SECOND SEMESTER. MODERN LITERATURE. 9:00 A.M.
WHAT DID YOU THINK OF THE INTRO FILM WILLIAMS SHOWED YESTERDAY?
I THOUGHT IT WAS A BRILLIANT KAFKAESQUE CRITIQUE OF BUREAUCRATIC COMPLEXITY IN PEDAGOGICAL SYSTEMS. I LOVED IT.
IT WAS ALMOST ORWELLIAN IN ITS REFLECTION OF THE DRACONIAN DOUBLESPEAK EMBLEMATIC OF THE ARTIST'S EARLY OEUVRE.
Kafkaesque
SEARCH
TAP TAP TAP
HELLO. I AM DR. QADRI LAKMALI. CALL ME QADRI. THIS CLASS IS NOT EASY, SO IF YOU AREN'T UP FOR A CHALLENGE THIS SEMESTER, YOU SHOULD LEAVE NOW.

ANYONE ELSE?
OK.

SQUEAK
SQUEAK

WITHOUT REFERENCING SILLY TELEPHONES, PLEASE WRITE THE DEFINITION OF *DOG* IN YOUR NOTEBOOKS.
TAP
WHAT. IS THE DEFINITION. OF *DOG*?

DOG...

DAY 1 of class JAN 10
kafkaesque

SCRATCH
SCRATCH
SCRATCH
SCRATCH

OK, THAT'S ENOUGH. NOW...YOU.
PLEASE TELL ME WHAT YOU WROTE DOWN.

AHEM...DOG: A MAMMAL WITH A SNOUT, CANINE TEETH, AND CLAWS.
CATS ALSO HAVE SNOUTS, CANINE TEETH, AND CLAWS. IS A CAT A DOG?

HMM...YOU.
A DOG IS A FOUR-LEGGED ANIMAL IN THE CANINE FAMILY.
YOU CAN'T VERY WELL USE *CANINE* IN THE DEFINITION OF *DOG*—IT'S LIKE DEFINING *MANGO* BY SAYING IT'S IN THE MANGO FAMILY.

JUDGMENT DAY.
YOU.
UM, I WROTE—
—"A DOG IS A MAMMAL THAT IS THE DOMESTICATED DESCENDANT OF A WOLF."

BUT NOT ALL DOGS ARE DOMESTICATED, ARE THEY? LET'S CLARIFY: TO DEFINE SOMETHING IS TO PUT BOUNDARIES AROUND IT.
EVERYTHING WITHIN MUST BE PERTINENT.
DOG
TAP

SO, NOW THAT WE KNOW *THAT*...PLEASE COULD SOMEONE TELL ME WHAT IS A DOG?
I WILL WAIT.

GOOD ENOUGH. PLEASE PASS AROUND THESE PACKETS, IF YOU WILL. NEXT WEEK WE ARE DISCUSSING JACQUES DERRIDA. PLEASE READ THIS THOROUGHLY. IF ANY OF YOU ARE FLUENT IN FRENCH, PLEASE READ IT IN ITS ORIGINAL LANGUAGE.

Ye Olde Shittee
Sarah
Maddy
January

Midwesterne Wintre
Liz
Jaysen
February

VALENTINE'S DAY.

I THINK A FUN, LIGHTHEARTED DEBATE ON THIS DAY OF LOVE IS IN ORDER. TAKE OUT YOUR COPIES OF *THE SEXUAL CONTRACT*, PLEASE.

I CAN'T BELIEVE I THOUGHT PAOLO WAS CUTER THAN GORDO. OR THAT HIS ACCENT WAS REAL.

I CAN'T BELIEVE WE THOUGHT IT WAS NORMAL FOR AN EIGHTH GRADER TO GO TO ROME AND IMMEDIATELY FIND A BOYFRIEND. SHE'S WHAT? THIRTEEN? HE'S GOTTA BE, LIKE, 16 AT THE YOUNGEST. THAT'S SO CREEPY.

I LOVE THIS MOVIE SO MUCH.
ME TOO.
YEAH.
I MISSED YOU GUYS. I FEEL LIKE I HAVEN'T SEEN YOU IN YEARS.
I'VE BEEN SO BUSY WITH WORK AND REHEARSALS, BUT IT STILL FEELS LIKE NOTHING EVER HAPPENS.

SLIP!
WIPE
WIPE
WIPE
WIPEOUT!

AND YOU'VE DONE THIS HOW MANY TIMES BEFORE?
DOZENS. I'VE BEEN CUTTING MY FRIENDS' HAIR FOR YEARS.
OH-KAY. I TRUST YOU.
IT'S A LITTLE DARK IN HERE. HMMM... SHOULD BE FINE.
BUZZZZZZZZ
OH-
BUZZT

YOU BITCH! YOU LIAR BITCH!

SO THE WHOLE SEASON IS ABOUT SOMEONE BEING INSECURE ABOUT HER RELATIONSHIPS AND MAKING IT EVERYONE ELSE'S PROBLEM?

WELL, NO, BUT ALSO, YES, KIND OF. IT GETS PRETTY DARK TOWARD THE END, WITH MARRIAGE AND ADDICTION AND FAMILY STUFF.

THE SHOW IS REALLY A STUDY OF EACH PERSON'S FATAL FLAWS. HAMARTIA, IF YOU WILL.

MID-MARCH, FRIDAY NIGHT.
CAN I LOOK?
OH! UM...
DOPE.
I'VE SEEN YOU AROUND ALL YEAR, ALWAYS DRAWING.
OH, YEAH, JUST...
...DRAWING.

THAT'S SICK.
MY BAD, I'M BRUNO.

SARAH. NICE TO MEET YOU!

HEY, ME AND SOME OF MY BUDDIES ARE HAVING A LITTLE GET-TOGETHER IN MY ROOM LATER IF YOU'D BE INTERESTED IN STOPPING BY. RENOVATED SIDE, 103. WE'RE JUST GONNA CHILL. Y'KNOW.

OH MY GOD.

UH, YEAH, I THINK I'M FREE!
OH MY GOD.

DOPE, SEE YOU AROUND TEN?
SWEET!

OH MY GOD.

I JUST GOT INVITED TO HANG OUT WITH THAT GROUP WE SEE ALL THE TIME IN THE DINING HALL.
TREES OF THE MIDWEST

THE ONES WITH THE PANTS AND HAIR AND STUFF?

YEAH, THE PANTS AND HAIR.

ARE YOU GONNA GO?
NORTHERN CATALPA
HAWTHORN
OHIO BUCKEYE
BLACK WALNUT
AMERICAN ELM
RED OAK

YEAH. I DON'T REALLY KNOW WHAT HE MEANT BY "A LITTLE GET-TOGETHER." LIKE, SHOULD I GET OUT OF MY PAJAMAS?

TREES OF THE MIDWEST
I THOUGHT THOSE WERE YOUR NORMAL CLOTHES.

YOU CHANGED.
I WAS...COLD?
DOPE.
COME IN, COME IN. EVERYONE, THIS IS SARAH.
HEY!
RIFLE RIFLE
POOF

SO, SARAH, ARE YOU FROM AROUND HERE?
OH, UH, NO, MILWAUKEE.

MILWAUKEE MILWAUKEE?
WELL, 12 MINUTES NORTH ON THE HIGHWAY. IT'S JUST EASIER TO SAY MILWAUKEE. ARE YOU FROM HERE?

YEP, SAINT PAUL.
OH, COOL. *SAINT PAUL* SAINT PAUL?
SPRINKLE

INDEED. ANYWAYS, THIS IS ROBBY, JAMES, ELIJAH, DANIEL, AND MARIA.

WOW! SO YOU ALL CAME HERE TOGETHER?

YEAH, YEAH. *WE* WENT TO THE SCHOOL OF ENVIRONMENTAL STUDIES TOGETHER.

IS THAT A COLLEGE?

NO, IT'S A SPECIALIZED HIGH SCHOOL. LIKE AN ARTS HIGH SCHOOL, Y'KNOW.
YEAH, OF COURSE.
I DO NOT KNOW.

WELL, ACTUALLY, JAMES AND ELIJAH DON'T GO TO THE U, BUT THEY LIVE JUST OFF CAMPUS WITH A FEW OF OUR OTHER BUDDIES WHO GO HERE. THEY'RE IN A BAND. PASSION SUCCESSION, IF YOU EVER HEARD OF THEM.
TAP
TAP

OH, NO, BUT THAT'S AWESOME. I'VE ALWAYS WANTED TO BE IN A BAND.

DO YOU LISTEN TO RADIO Q?
ROLL
ROLL
UH, NO, NOT REALLY.

THEY PLAY THEIR STUFF ALL THE TIME. MARIA AND DANIEL ARE D.J.S AT THE STATION.

TUESDAYS AND THURSDAYS AT 1:00 A.M.
OVERNIGHT SHIFT.

I DIDN'T EVEN KNOW THAT WAS A JOB HERE.
THAT'S SO SICK.

I SEE YOU DRAWING ALL THE TIME IN THE BUILDING. YOU SEEM LIKE YOU'RE ALWAYS WORKING ON SOMETHING.
ARE YOU AN ART STUDENT?

NO, I'M JUST TAKING SOME CLASSES.
MOSTLY DOCUMENTING MY PATHETIC LITTLE LIFE.

CHUCKLE
FLICK

I WOULD TEAR OFF MY SKIN IF YOU ASKED ME TO.

HEY, WE'RE GONNA BE AT THE SEWER TOMORROW NIGHT IF YOU'RE AROUND.
DISCO MUSIC, DANCING, BOX WINE.
REAL CHILL.
THE SEWER?
JAMES AND ELIJAH'S PLACE. IT'S A BASEMENT. LOTS OF PIPES. WE CALL IT THE SEWER.
YOU CAN WALK WITH US—WE'RE LEAVING AROUND 11.
THE NEXT DAY, BEFORE MADDY'S PLAY.
I GUESS THEY HANG OUT THERE ALL THE TIME AND PLAY DISCO MUSIC AND DANCE AND STUFF.
SNIP
SNIP
SOUNDS LIKE FUN.
YEAH, THEY'RE SO NICE! MOST OF THEM ARE VEGAN, TOO. I THINK I'M GOING TO JOIN THE PRINT CLUB. MARIA SAID THEY HAVE GUESTS AND GET FREE ART SUPPLIES.
ALSO, THEY ASKED IF I WANTED TO SMOKE WITH THEM ON THE TRAIN TRACKS BUT DIDN'T MAKE ME FEEL WEIRD WHEN I DIDN'T WANT TO. IT WAS AWESOME.
GREAT.

ARE YOU FEELING OK?

WELL, I THOUGHT WE WERE GOING TO HANG OUT AFTER MADDY'S PLAY SINCE SHE'S GOING TO A CAST PARTY TONIGHT.

OH, I FIGURED YOU HAD YOUR OWN PLANS SINCE YOU'RE NEVER HOME...
DO YOU WANT TO COME TO THE SEWER WITH ME?

I CAN MAKE MY OWN PLANS.

HEY! THANKS FOR COMING! I'M SO GLAD YOU MADE IT.
OF COURSE, THAT'S WHAT FRIENDS ARE FOR.

YOU WERE GREAT! I LIKED YOUR TUTU.
THANKS!
SO SORRY, BUT I CAN'T STICK AROUND TOO LONG. MY DAD AND FRANK ARE IN TOWN, AND I HAVE TO MAKE SURE TO GET TO THEM BEFORE THEY HEAD BACK TO THEIR HOTEL.
I'LL SEE YOU GUYS LATER, THOUGH!

HAVE A GOOD NIGHT.
YEP.

SARAAAHH!
FRANCIA
VINO
JUST A CRUSH.
IT'S JUST A CRUSH.

MEN
WOMEN
MEN
WOMEN
SIT FOR A MOMENT, AND THINK OF EVERY PEJORATIVE TERM YOU CAN FOR MEN AND WOMEN SEPARATELY. OK? OK.
READY? I WILL BEGIN TO BREAK THE ICE.
BITCH

SLUT.

DICK.
WHORE.
HAG.
SHREW.
BIMBO.

TWENTY MINUTES LATER.
MEN
RELATION/ COMPARISON TO WOMEN (ALSO INSULTS WOMEN)
WOMEN

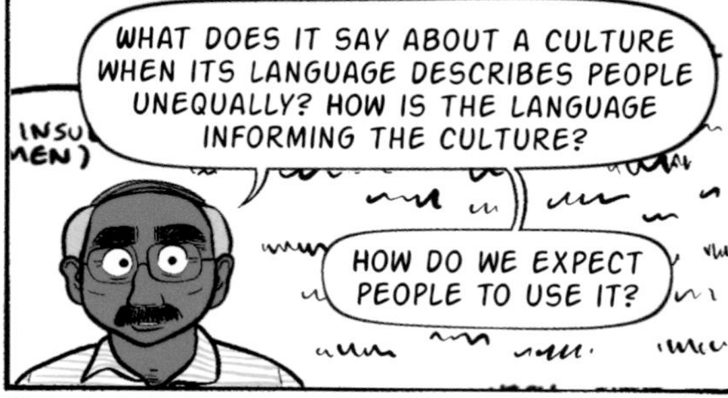
WHAT DOES IT SAY ABOUT A CULTURE WHEN ITS LANGUAGE DESCRIBES PEOPLE UNEQUALLY? HOW IS THE LANGUAGE INFORMING THE CULTURE?
HOW DO WE EXPECT PEOPLE TO USE IT?

FLATTEN

=SIGH=

BUZZ
BUZZ
BUZZ
BUZZ

HEY, YOU!
IT'S BEEN SO LONG. I MISSED YOU.

I MISSED YOU, TOO.
DO YOU HAVE A MINUTE?
YEAH, WHAT'S UP?
ARE YOU OK?

YEAH, I'M FINE.
I JUST NEEDED TO TELL YOU SOMETHING. I DON'T WANT YOU TO GET UPSET...

SCIENCE MATTERS
EARTH DAY
CLIMATE STRIKE
2016
TRUTH MATTERS
I WON'T.

FINN AND I TALKED, AND WE THOUGHT IT WOULD BE BETTER FOR US TO TELL YOU THAN FOR YOU TO FIND OUT ON YOUR OWN.

...OK.
SILVER MAPLE
RED PINE
TRUTH

SO...BEN AND AMELIE STARTED DATING A COUPLE OF WEEKS AGO.
WHAT?

I KNOW YOU GUYS HAVE BEEN FRIENDLY AND STUFF, SO I JUST WANTED YOU TO HEAR FROM ME BEFORE YOU SAW ANYTHING ONLINE.

HOW DOES THAT EVEN LOGISTICALLY MAKE SENSE? I—
RUB
RUB

WELL, THEY'VE BEEN FRIENDS FOR A COUPLE OF YEARS. I GUESS THEY JUST THOUGHT THEY'D TRY IT OUT.

WHA–? I–I LITERALLY JUST TALKED TO HIM ON THE PHONE LAST WEEK ABOUT PHOTO STUFF.
WHAT?

HE SAID YOU GUYS WERE SUPER CHILL. ALSO, SINCE AMELIE WAS GONE AT CAMP MOST OF THE SUMMER, SHE DIDN'T REALIZE YOU GUYS HAD BEEN SO SERIOUS.

HE SAID WE COULD TRY GETTING BACK TOGETHER WHEN I GOT HOME.
WHEN DID HE SAY THAT?

WHEN WE BROKE UP.

...FIVE MONTHS AGO?

BUR OAK
HAWTHORN
PINE
- TRUTH
...YEAH?

SARAH...HE STARTED DATING OTHER PEOPLE A WEEK AFTER YOU BROKE UP.
HE *DID?*

I DIDN'T WANT TO TELL YOU THIS, BUT...HE CAME TO THE THANKSGIVING THING BECAUSE HE WANTED TO SEE AMELIE.

OH MY GOD–

I'M SORRY, SARAH. I THOUGHT YOU WERE OVER HIM! YOU SEEMED LIKE YOU'RE HAVING SO MUCH FUN AT SCHOOL.
I-I'M N-NOT! IT-IT S-SUCKS! I'M S-SO LONELY ***ALL TH-THE T-TIME.***

I'M SORRY. I DIDN'T KNOW. I'VE BARELY HEARD FROM YOU IN MONTHS. I JUST THOUGHT YOU WERE BUSY AND DOING BETTER SINCE YOU'VE BEEN POSTING SO MUCH ART.

SPRUCE
SILVER MAPLE
HAWTHORN
PINE
I-I DON'T M-MAKE A-ART WHEN I'M H-HAPPY!

WELL, I'M SORRY. I WISH YOU HAD TOLD ME— I WOULDN'T HAVE SAID ANYTHING.
Y-YOU KNEW? YOU ALL **KNEW** THIS W-WHOLE TIME AND DIDN'T SAY ANYTHING?

WE THOUGHT IT WAS THE RIGHT THING TO DO.
DID YOU KNOW THAT HE WAS GOING TO D-DUMP ME, TOO?

WELL...
KITCHEN STUFF
BATH
TO DO LIST:
TREES OF THE MIDWEST
BUR OAK
SILVER MAPLE
HAWTHORN
SCIENCE MATTERS
EARTH DAY
CLIMATE STRIKE
·2016·
-TRUTH MATTERS-

SUCKS
SARAH
SARAH SUCKS
SHE
THINGS
SARAH
SUCKS
IS BAD
IS THE WORST
FOR MANY REASONS
FOREVER
WHO SUCKS?
SARAH
AND BEN HATES YOU AND AMELIE HATES YOU AND EMMA HATES YOU AND FINN HATES YOU AND I HATE YOU...
B- NOT YOUR BEST
J'AI ÉTÉ, TU AS ÉTÉ, NOUS AVONS ÉTÉ...
STUDY AT MY PLACE LATER?
I'M STAYING IN TONIGHT. I HAVE TO CATCH UP ON SOME READING. I'LL TEXT YOU.

SCIENCE MATTERS
EARTH DAY
THE BAKERS ARE NOW CHALLENGED TO IMPRESS THE JUDGES WITH THEIR DEPRESSION CAKES. YOU HAVE TWO HOURS.
BUZZ BUZZ BUZZ BUZZ
SORRY, SARAH CAN'T COME TO THE PHONE RIGHT NOW. SHE HAS ENTERED THE VOID. PLEASE TRY TO REACH HER AT A LATER DATE. TIME ISN'T REAL. BEEP!
BUZZ-T
6:52pm
Friday
Sewer tonight?
CLICK

OH, HEY.
WERE YOU SITTING IN THE DARK?
MMM.

ARE YOU OK?
MM-HMM.

HAVE YOU EATEN TODAY?
MM-HMM.

WHAT DID YOU EAT?
GRANOLA BAR.

THAT'S NOT FOOD, SARAH. COME EAT DINNER WITH ME.

MMM.

ARE YOU SURE YOU DON'T WANT TO EAT ANYTHING ELSE? THAT'S NOT THAT MUCH, SARAH.
MM-HMM.
YOU NEED PROTEIN.
PICK PICK

I'M GONNA GO GET YOU SOME SOUP.
200
HERE. FOOD.

OK. ARE YOU GOING TO TELL ME WHAT'S WRONG?
I'M FINE.
I'LL GET OVER IT.

YOU LOOK KIND OF PALE. I DON'T THINK YOU'RE EATING ENOUGH. MAYBE YOU SHOULD TAKE A LITTLE BREAK FROM THE RAW VEGAN THING.
WHAT ABOUT CEREAL?

SO, ANY PLANS TONIGHT?
THE SEWER. I NEED TO NAP BEFORE I GO. I'M REALLY TIRED.

ARE YOU SURE YOU'RE FEELING UP TO THAT?

WHATEVER.

THUMP
THUMP
THUMP
THUMP
THUMP
THUMP

HOW DO YOU KNOW BRUNO?
THUMP
THU

WHAT?
HOW DO YOU KNOW BRUNO?

OH, THE DORMS.
THE DORMS.
THUMP
THUMP
OH, COOL.
THUMP
TH

AREN'T THEY CUTE?
WHO?

ROBBY AND HIS GIRLFRIEND.
HIS GIRLFRIEND?

YEAH, THEY'VE BEEN DATING SINCE SOPHOMORE YEAR.
OF HIGH SCHOOL?

AND IT'S, LIKE, I FEEL LIKE I'M DISAPPOINTING EVERYONE.
HIC
I THINK I'M SCREWING EVERYTHING UP, AND WHEN I COME-
HIC
-HOME THIS YEAR, EVERYONE IS GOING TO THINK I'M A LOSER BECAUSE I HAD A BAD TIME, YOU KNOW?
HIC
I GET IT.
I FEEL LIKE I CAN'T GET FRIENDS TO STAY AROUND FOR MORE THAN, LIKE, A YEAR. SINCE MIDDLE SCHOOL. HIC IT'S LIKE EVERYBODY HATES ME. I CAN NEVER SAY THE RIGHT THING. EVEN MY DOG, HE DOESN'T EVEN REALLY LIKE ME.
I DON'T HATE YOU.

SMOOCH!
MACK!
SMACK!
SON OF A—

SATURDAY MORNING, 7:30.
BEEP BEEP BEEP BEEP
SHIFT SHIFT SHIFT
SARAHHHH, INCREDIBLE MOVES ON THE DANCE FLOOR LAST NIGHT.
SO WHAT'S HAPPENING WITH HIM? ARE YOU GUYS A THING NOW?
NO. HE HAS A GIRLFRIEND. LONG-TERM. SHE'S REALLY PRETTY.

THAT SUCKS.
IT'S OK.
I KISSED SOME GUY LAST NIGHT.
YOU DID?
WHO?
PICK PICK
YOU'LL NEVER BELIEVE WHAT HIS NAME IS.
SHIFT SHIFT
WHAT?
BEN. WHAT A SICK TWIST OF FATE.
OOF. SORRY.
SHIFT
I THINK I MIGHT JUST... NOT GO OUT FOR A MINUTE.

BAD FRIEND

HEY, UH... I'M SORRY WE HAVEN'T HUNG OUT THAT MUCH LATELY. THINGS HAVE BEEN... CHAOTIC.

NO, I MEAN, ME TOO. I'VE BEEN REALLY TIED UP WITH WORK AND SCHOOL AND ALL THE CLUBS. IT'S TOO MUCH. I'M SO GLAD SPRING BREAK IS NEXT WEEK, OR I THINK I'D COLLAPSE.
YEAH, I FEEL YOU.

APPLY TODAY!
/HR
UM, WOULD YOU WANNA GO TO THE MINI-TARGET WITH ME? I NEED TO GET SOME...STUFF.

MY MOM SAID TO CALL HER WHEN THIS HAPPENS, BUT I JUST GOOGLED IT, AND IT SAID I NEED...
OVERNIGHT SANITARY NAPKINS
MAXI PADS
X-TRA THIN PADS
PAIN RELIEF
COOLING ~ OINTMENT
MONISTAT
ANTI FUNGAL
PREGNANCY TEST
FAST RELIEF
ITCHING, BURNING AND IRRITATION
MEDICATED CREME
Vagisil
HELLO WORLD
VAGISIL
LOOK AT ME! I HAVE A YEAST INFECTION!
SHIT SHIT SHIT!
WHAT?
WHAT?

UH...I JUST NEED A FEW MORE THINGS.

BEEP
BEEP
BEEP

SEE YOU AROUND.
BEN

YEP. THIS WILL SOLVE ALL MY PROBLEMS!

SPRING BREAK!

SPRING BREAK.

WHEN I FIRST STARTED DATING YOUR DAD, I WENT THROUGH THIS WHOLE PURPLE PHASE. PURPLE COAT, PURPLE SHOES, PURPLE BAG— EVERYTHING. I TRIED TINTING MY HAIR RED, BUT IT TURNED COMPLETELY MAROON. THAT NIGHT, I WAS MEETING YOUR DAD AT A BODEGA, AND I WAS STANDING UNDER THIS BIG BLUE COORS LITE NEON SIGN, AND I LOOKED LIKE A HUGE GRAPE.
ANYWAYS, I THINK THE HAIR IS CUTE. GET IT OUT OF YOUR SYSTEM NOW WHILE YOU CAN.

YEAH, I REMEMBER THAT STORY. IT'S FUNNY.
STAB
STAB

SO WHAT'S NEW?
ANYTHING INTERESTING?

I HAVE A CRUSH.
YOU DO?

JUST A GUY FROM MY DORM. HE'S CUTE.
BUT HE HAS A GIRLFRIEND.

DON'T MESS WITH THAT. JUST STAY FOCUSED ON YOUR WORK.
SCHOOL FIRST.

WELL, I COULD NEVER DATE HIM ANYWAY BECAUSE HE'S NAMED ROBERT, AND I COULD NEVER GO FOR SOMEONE NAMED ROBERT—
EVEN IF I REALLY WANTED TO.

...I COULD SEE THAT BEING WEIRD.
SCRATCH
SCRATCH

SO...I TOOK HUEY TO THE VET LAST WEEK.
OK...

YOU KNOW HOW HE'S ALWAYS LICKING THAT LEG?
DR. BROWN FOUND A TUMOR.

WHAT DOES THAT MEAN?

IT'S MALIGNANT, BUT THEY THINK HE'S GOING TO BE OK. WE HAVE TO START HIM ON SOME MEDICATIONS NEXT WEEK.
IT'S LIKE DOGGO CHEMO.

DREADED ANNUAL CHECKUP.
Welcome to Pediatrics!
Welcome to
SARAH?
rics!
NOT COMING IN ANYMORE
DOESN'T KNOW HOW INSURANCE WORKS

INHALE
EXHALE
CLICK
CLICK
PATIENT HEALTH QUESTIONAIRE
NAME
DATE
GRAND TOTAL:

CRINKLE
CRINKLE
DON'T LOOK AT ME LIKE THAT.
PROD
PROD

YOU'RE 18 NOW, SO I'M GOING TO SET YOU UP FOR AN APPOINTMENT WITH A GYNECOLOGIST FOR YOUR FIRST PELVIC EXAM, OK? I AM ALSO GOING TO GET YOU SET UP WITH A NEW PRIMARY CARE PHYSICIAN. NO MORE PEDIATRICS.
OK.

AND ALL YOUR MEDICATIONS ARE STILL CURRENT: BIRTH CONTROL, CLARITIN, EPIPEN, OCCASIONAL ALBUTEROL, AND STEROID CREAMS?
YEP.
TAP TAP TA

OK...JUST SOME QUICK QUESTIONS. ANY DRINKING OR SMOKING?
NOT REALLY AND NO.

ARE YOU SEXUALLY ACTIVE?
NOT...RECENTLY.
OK...
TAP TAP TA
TAP TA

SARAH, HAVE YOU EVER CONSIDERED TRYING ANTIDEPRESSANTS?

DO YOU WANT TO TALK ABOUT IT?
NO.
SOMETIMES I WONDER WHAT IT WOULD'VE BEEN LIKE IF THE LAST FEW YEARS HAD GONE DIFFERENTLY...
NO, MOM—
I KNOW TIMES WERE TOUGH. I WISH I COULD HAVE BEEN THERE FOR YOU MORE.

YOU WERE.
YOU DID THE BEST YOU COULD.
I JUST MISS MY HAPPY LITTLE GIRL. WHERE DID SHE GO?
ARE
SSRIs

THE NEXT DAY.

I HAVEN'T SEEN A LITTLE KID IN MONTHS. I SAW ONE YESTERDAY, AND IT KIND OF FREAKED ME OUT. I JUST TOTALLY FORGOT ABOUT THEM.

I BET.

AND IT'S SO NICE TO SHOWER AT HOME. AND NOT HAVING EVERYONE ON YOUR FLOOR HEAR YOU PEE. THE BATHROOMS ARE SO ECHOEY.

IT'S SADISTIC.

I GUESS THAT'S ONE BENEFIT OF LIVING ALONE— I DON'T REALLY WORRY ABOUT THAT.

REMEMBER AFTER GRADUATION WHEN WE STAYED UP ALL NIGHT IN MY PARENTS' BACKYARD AND THEN CAME HERE AND WATCHED THE SUNRISE OVER THIS BLUFF? WE WERE SO TIRED THE NEXT DAY AT WORK.

HAH HAH
YEAH. THAT WAS GREAT.

I'M NOT MAD AT YOU ABOUT THE BEN STUFF, BY THE WAY.

I PROBABLY SHOULD'VE JUST TOLD YOU RIGHT AWAY, BUT I DIDN'T WANT TO HURT YOUR FEELINGS. I DIDN'T KNOW YOU STILL FELT THAT WAY ABOUT HIM.

NO, YOU WERE RIGHT. I PROBABLY WOULD HAVE DONE THE SAME THING. HONESTLY, I DIDN'T EVEN KNOW I STILL FELT THAT WAY. IT ALL SEEMS KINDA STUPID NOW.
SPEAKING OF WHICH...

DING DONG
HEY!
HEY.
SORRY FOR THE SHORT NOTICE.
I'M NOT HOME FOR LONG. I JUST THOUGHT—
NO, NO! NO PROBLEM.
COOL, UM...

WELL, I BETTER-
SO HOW ARE YOU-

SORRY, I DIDN'T-
OH, YEAH, OF COURSE-

HEY, LOOK. UM, I DON'T WANT THINGS TO BE WEIRD. WE'RE ALL GOOD.

OH, I DIDN'T KNOW THINGS WER-
YOU HAVE MY JACKET?

OH!
OH, YEAH, HERE YOU GO.

SO...
...HOW'S SCHOOL GOING?
HONESTLY?
KIND OF TERRIBLE.
YOU?
HONESTLY?
SAME.

LAST DAYS OF MARCH.

NEXT WEEK, PLEASE BRING YOUR COPIES OF DERRIDA BACK TO CLASS.

WE WILL BE REEVALUATING THE TEXT USING OUR NEW UNDERSTANDING OF THE EPISTEME.

FIRST DAYS OF APRIL.

CAN I TALK TO YOU ABOUT SOMETHING?

YEAH, SURE.

IT'S JUST...NOT WHAT I WANTED IT TO BE. I THOUGHT I WAS GOING TO BE DOING ALL THIS ***"THEATER,"*** BUT IT'S MOSTLY WALKING AROUND IN RECTANGLES FAST AND SLOW AND A LOT OF GOSSIP AND HIERARCHIES. I JUST WANTED TO BE IN PLAYS. LAST WEEK, MY HOMEWORK WAS TO "DISCOVER MY SPINE."

YOU CAN ONLY ROLL UP VERTEBRA BY VERTEBRA SO MANY TIMES...

I THINK I JUST EXPECTED SOMETHING DIFFERENT. BUT NOW I HAVE TO FIGURE OUT HOW TO TAKE ENOUGH CREDITS TO KEEP MY SCHOLARSHIP, AND THERE'S ALL THESE EMAILS TO THE FINANCIAL AID OFFICE, AND PHONE CALLS AND MEETINGS, AND IT'S SO...UGH.
ALSO, I LOST MY DEBIT CARD LAST WEEK DURING A FIRE DRILL AT 3:00 A.M., AND IT TAKES TEN DAYS TO GET A NEW ONE.

THAT SOUNDS STRESSFUL. I'M SORRY.
YEAH, IT SUCKS. ANYWAYS, RANT OVER. HOW IS YOUR STUFF GOING?

WELL, YOU KNOW HOW I WAS THINKING OF TRANSFERRING TO AN ART SCHOOL BEFORE WINTER BREAK? I'M JUST GOING TO STICK IT OUT HERE.

OH! THAT'S GOOD! THAT'S GOOD? HOW ARE WE FEELING ABOUT THAT?

I APPLIED TO ART SCHOOLS LAST YEAR, BUT I WAS TOO SCARED TO ACTUALLY GO. IT KINDA FELT LIKE DECIDING NOT TO DO ART SCHOOL WAS LIKE DECIDING NOT TO BE AN ARTIST, BUT I DON'T REALLY FEEL THAT WAY ANYMORE.

NO, I GET IT. WHEN I FIRST CAME HERE, I THOUGHT IT WAS THE WRONG CHOICE, TOO. LIKE I SHOULD'VE AIMED HIGHER OR SOMETHING.

YOU'RE AN HONORS STUDENT WITH A SCHOLARSHIP. YOU AIMED PRETTY HIGH.
WELL...YOU KNOW. IVYS OR WHATEVER.

LISTEN, I KNOW A COUPLE OF PEOPLE WHO GOT INTO IVYS, AND I DON'T THINK THEY'RE ANY HAPPIER THAN THE REST OF US. ALSO, THEY'RE THE WORST.
HA.
YEAH.

IT'S JUST FUNNY HOW WE ALL DID SO DIFFERENTLY IN HIGH SCHOOL, AND WE ALL ENDED UP HERE. I GOT A C- IN GEOMETRY SOPHOMORE YEAR, AND I'M IN THE SAME COLLEGE AS YOU. IT'S ALMOST LIKE NONE OF IT MATTERED.
SOME OF IT MUST HAVE MATTERED.

A.P. SPANISH.
YEAH, THAT DAMN A.P. SPANISH.

BUT THESE ARE SUPPOSED TO BE THE BEST YEARS OF MY LIFE? IT SEEMS LIKE EVERYBODY IS HAVING A GREAT TIME EXCEPT ME.
THAT MAKES TWO OF US.
BE VULNERABLE
MAKE A JOKE
WELL, I'M HAPPY I MET YOU. YOU'RE A REALLY GOOD FRIEND.
HONESTLY, MAYBE SELFISHLY, I'M HAPPY YOU'RE STAYING.
YEAH, ME TOO.
GOD, HOW IS THE YEAR ALMOST OVER ALREADY? HOW DID THAT EVEN HAPPEN?
THE ACADEMIC WORLD IS A TIME WARP.

I DON'T WANT TO TAKE THIS QUIZ. I WISH I COULD USE MY GREASY SIDE BANGS TO FLY AWAY.
MAYBE IF I LOOK PATHETIC ENOUGH, FARIDA WILL COME OVER AND DO THE THING WHERE SHE ASKS YOU QUESTIONS UNTIL SHE ESSENTIALLY TELLS YOU THE ANSWER.
I WOULDN'T BANK ON THAT. I THINK WE'VE USED UP ALL HER EMPATHY FOR THE REST OF THE SEMESTER.
HA.
SO HOW'S THE INTERNSHIP GOING? I HAVEN'T SEEN YOU IN FOREVER.
IT'S...FINE. I FEEL KIND OF SILLY NOW, BUT I THOUGHT BEING AN ARTIST'S ASSISTANT WAS GOING TO BE A LITTLE BIT MORE ABOUT THE... ***ART?*** I MOSTLY UPDATE HIS WEBSITE AND PACKAGE BOOK ORDERS AND HANG LIGHTS. IT'S GREAT, IT'S JUST...NOT WHAT I THOUGHT IT WAS GOING TO BE.
THAT'S TOO BAD.
EH, IT'S OK. I'M PAYING MY DUES TO THE ART WORLD OR WHATEVER THEY SAY. DID I EVER SHOW YOU HOW MY FILM SERIES TURNED OUT?

JAYSEN'S PROJECT.
THEY'RE NOT QUITE DONE YET, BUT I LIKE HOW THEY'RE TURNING OUT. I'M IN A GALLERY SHOW HERE IN A COUPLE OF WEEKS. GRAPES, CRACKERS, CHEESE. THAT KIND OF THING.
I'LL BE THERE.

SARAH'S PROJECT.
WOW, THIS IS REALLY... LONG. WHAT WAS THE ASSIGNMENT?
A 30-SECOND ANIMATION.

SARAH, THIS IS TWO AND A HALF MINUTES LONG.
I'VE NEVER BEEN VERY GOOD AT KEEPING THINGS SIMPLE.

HOW TO RATION EMOTIONAL ENERGY

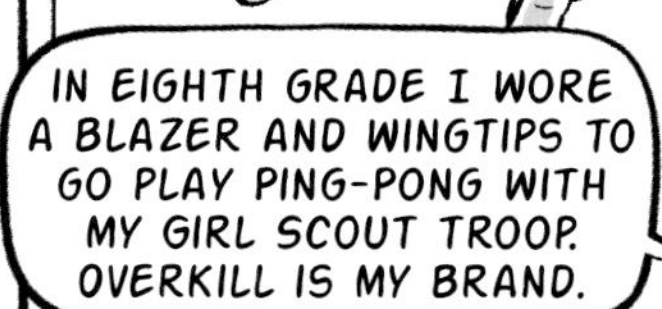
HOW SARAH RATIONS EMOTIONAL ENERGY
IN EIGHTH GRADE I WORE A BLAZER AND WINGTIPS TO GO PLAY PING-PONG WITH MY GIRL SCOUT TROOP. OVERKILL IS MY BRAND.

WELL, YEAH. THE ONLY WEIRD PART IS THAT SHE LOOKS JUST LIKE ME. GLASSES, HAIR, THE WHOLE THING. WE EVEN USED TO DRESS ALIKE.

OOF. ATTACK OF THE DOPPELGANGER.

NOW I JUST WRITE ABOUT DEATH.

A REGULAR OLD TUESDAY.
I HOPE I NEVER HAVE TO READ JOHN LOCKE EVER AGAIN.
I HOPE I NEVER HAVE TO DO CHEM MODULES EVER AGAIN.
WANNA TRADE? I COULD GET YOU AN F IF I REALLY TRIED.
HA.
HEY, IT'LL ALL BE WORTH IT WHEN YOU'RE A FANCY ENGINEER AT SOME FIRM MAKING SIX FIGURES.
YEAH, WELL...I'M DROPPING OUT OF THE ENGINEERING PROGRAM.
WHAT?
I HATE IT. AND FOR WHAT? SO I CAN MAKE A BUNCH OF MONEY PUMPING TOXIC CHEMICALS INTO THE WATERWAYS FOR ANOTHER 100 YEARS? I CAN'T TAKE IT ANYMORE.
SO...
...WHAT'S THE PLAN NOW?

I STILL HAVE TO TELL MY MOM. SHE AND MY STEPDAD ARE GOING TO BE PISSED. THEY WERE SO HAPPY WHEN I GOT INTO THE PROGRAM. THANK GOD MY CLASSES WERE ALL SCIENCE PREREQUISITES OR I WOULD'VE WASTED THE LOAN I TOOK OUT THIS YEAR.

RUB RUB

IF THEY ***ARE*** PISSED, WHICH I DON'T THINK THEY ***WILL*** BE, I WILL BAKE YOU A TRAY OF BROWNIES–

–AND WE CAN EAT THE ENTIRE THING AND WATCH *THE SPONGEBOB MOVIE* AS MANY TIMES AS YOU WANT.

I THINK IT'S A REALLY GREAT IDEA, LIZ.

ALSO, MY PARENTS WOULD BE OVERJOYED IF I TOLD THEM I WAS GOING TO STUDY SCIENCE AND POLICY INSTEAD OF ENGLISH.

I JUST...I SAW YOU WITH YOUR NEW FRIENDS, AND I FELT LIKE...YOU'RE GOOD AT MAKING FRIENDS, AND I'M BASICALLY ONLY FRIENDS WITH THE PEOPLE I CAME HERE WITH.

THAT'S NOT TRUE. YOU'RE THE ONE WHO JOINED ALL THE CLUBS AND GOT A COOL JOB AND STUFF. I CAN'T EVEN TAKE THE BUS ALONE WITHOUT FREAKING OUT.

I'M A COWARD.

SO? WILL YOU COME?
YOU COULD KEEP ME AWAY FROM ANY STRAY BENS THAT MIGHT WANDER MY WAY.
THAT'S NOT A BAD IDEA.
YOU CAN'T GET HEARTBROKEN AGAIN BECAUSE I DON'T KNOW HOW MUCH MORE ALANIS MORISSETTE I CAN HANDLE.
DEAL. NO BENS. NO PROBLEM. LESS ALANIS.
AT LEAST WHEN YOU'RE HOME.
YOU KNOW WHAT? I *WILL* COME WITH YOU.
IT'LL BE FUN.
EEEEE!
HA HA HA.

JAYSEN'S GALLERY.
LOOK, I'M JUST SAYING, YOU CAN'T TRUST INDIE PUNK ARTISTS WITH PERFECT TEETH. IT'S THE TRUTH.
THE SERIES I CREATED THIS SEMESTER IS MEANT TO INVESTIGATE QUEER DESIRE AND QUEER ISOLATION.
THE FOLLOWING IS FROM MY ESSAY "INTIMACY AND LONELINESS"–
"LONELINESS IS TO REACH FROM THE SELF AND NEVER GRASP.
"TO PUSH AND PULL, TO INDULGE AND BE UNFULFILLED, TO BE CLOSE AND FEEL ALONE.
"TO ACTIVELY WANT WHAT YOU WILL NOT LET YOURSELF HAVE.
"WE ARE SO FOCUSED ON LIBERATING OURSELVES THROUGH SEX THAT WE FORGET TO STOP AND ASK IF IT'S HELPING."

FINAL FINALS.
TAP TAP TAP TAP TAP TAP TAP TAP TAP TAP TAP TAP TAP T
TAP TAP TAP T
TAP TAP TAP TAP TAP
1:48am
TAP
BEEP BEEP BEEP BEEP BEEP BEEP BEEP BEEP BEEP BE
SNORE
GROAN
HAVE YOU BEEN HERE ALL NIGHT?

HA! YEAH, I HAVE ONE MORE DAY, EIGHT MORE PAGES. I CAN...I JUST NEED SOME TOAST.
I THINK YOU NEED MORE THAN TOAST, SARAH.
ZZZzzzzzzzz
TAP TAP TAP
TAP TAP TAP TAP
Page 15 of 15
TWITCH

HEHEHE.
NORTH HIGH SCHOOL
NORTH HIGH SCHOOL
HEHEHE.
HEHEHE.
CLICK
CLICK
CLICK
CLICK
ZZZZZZ
HAHAHA
CLICK
NORTH HIGH SCHOOL TOUR
HS COLLEGE TOUR
CLICK
YOU KNOW THIS ONLY HAD TO BE 30 SECONDS, RIGHT?
CLICK!
SUBMIT

WELL...
...WE SHOULD PROBABLY START PACKING.
I GUESS SO.
FINISH FINALS!!
TREES OF THE MIDWEST
SCIENCE MATTERS
EARTH DAY CLIMATE STRIKE 2016
TRUTH MATTERS
THE SpongeBob SquarePants MOVIE

I CAN'T BELIEVE I'M NOT SICK RIGHT NOW. MUST HAVE BEEN DIVINE INTERVENTION.
I KNOW. I DIDN'T THINK I WAS GOING TO MAKE IT THROUGH MY LAST STUDIO.
LAST DAY ON CAMPUS.
I'M GONNA MISS YOU THIS SUMMER.
GROSS.
I'M GONNA MISS YOU, TOO.
IF YOU EVER NEED TO ESCAPE YOUR PARENTS OR EX-BOYFRIENDS AND COME BACK HERE, LET ME KNOW.
HAH
WE COULD DO A SLEEPOVER LIKE THE GOOD OLD DAYS. *HOUSEWIVES*, PASTA, THE WHOLE THING.
I'M GONNA BE A LIFEGUARD.
HOW BAD COULD MY SUMMER BE?
THANKS, GUYS! I'LL SEE YOU IN MILWAUKEE!
MAKE SURE TO TEXT ME ABOUT SUMMERFEST.

TO DO:
MOVE TF OUT!!
HOW DID YOU COME BACK WITH SO MUCH MORE STUFF?
GOOD QUESTION.

SHE'S HOME! WAHOOOOO!

JUST PUSH IT ONTO THE FLOOR.
SOME THINGS NEVER CHANGE.

SARAH, YOUR BIRTHDAY IS COMING UP THIS MONTH, SO WE PLANNED A LITTLE SURPRISE. WELL, TWO SURPRISES, ACTUALLY.
AWWW, YOU GUYS DIDN'T HAVE TO DO ANYTHING! TELL ME, TELL ME.

SO YOU KNOW HOW I'M LEAVING FOR NEW YORK NEXT WEEK?
YEAH...
RIFLE

GUESS WHO'S COMING WITH?
WAIT, WHAT?

THEY'RE STANDBY TICKETS, BUT MY DAD SAID THE CHANCES OF US GETTING ON THE PLANE ARE PRETTY HIGH. WELL, FIFTY-FIFTY. EITHER WAY, YOU CAN THANK CAPTAIN TONY FOR THESE. ALSO, IT'S ONLY TWO AND A HALF DAYS AND THE APARTMENT ISN'T FURNISHED, BUT IT'LL BE GREAT!

NO, THAT'S PERFECT!
THE OTHER SURPRISE IS FROM ME. DON'T BE MAD.

WHY WOULD I BE MAD? WHAT, ARE *YOU* DATING BEN NOW?
HA HA.
NO. I'M MOVING TO AUSTRALIA!
IN JUNE!

ARE YOU JOKING?
I FINALLY FOUND THE RIGHT YOUTH TRAVEL AND WORK PROGRAM. I'M ALWAYS TALKING ABOUT DOING IT, AND I DECIDED I'M ACTUALLY GOING, THE SOONER THE BETTER.

I'LL WORK AT A RESTAURANT IN SYDNEY AND TRAVEL ON THE WEEKENDS.

THAT'S...AMAZING.
WOW, EMMA, THAT'S SO COOL.
I KNOW! THAT'S WHY I WAS THINKING WE SHOULD GO VISIT FINN IN NEW YORK, AS A FINAL HOORAH.
WOW, YOU GUYS, I JUST—
—I'M REALLY GLAD YOU'RE BOTH DOING THIS. WE'RE, LIKE, GROWN UP.
HEY, MOM, CAN I GO TO NEW YORK WITH FINN AND EMMA THIS WEEKEND? NO, **NEW YORK.**

THE FINAL HOORAH.
PHARMACY
WE'RE STILL WORKING ON THE FURNITURE PART.
NO, IT'S GREAT, I LOVE IT!
AND THE BEST PART...
OH MY GOD.

I KNOW, RIGHT?
SHAKE
SHAKE
TAP

UH...WHAT HAPPENED TO "I'M NEVER GONNA SMOKE"?
FLICK
FLICK

SHRUG
EH, PEOPLE CHANGE.

WAKEY WAKEY!

UGGHHH.
IT'S SO HOT IN HERE.
5:10
TAP

IT'S GONNA BE 103 DEGREES TODAY.
I HOPE YOU PACKED SHORTS!

MY HEAD IS POUNDING. I THINK I ONLY SLEPT FOR, LIKE, THREE HOURS LAST NIGHT.
YOU'RE ONLY HERE FOR ONE MORE DAY. LESS, ACTUALLY.
YOU **SHOULD** ONLY SLEEP FOR THREE HOURS.

SPEAKING OF WHICH, IF I SIT NEXT TO THE THEATER OVERNIGHT, I CAN GET US DISCOUNTED RUSH TICKETS FOR A B-RATED MUSICAL.
YOU CAN'T **SLEEP** IN TIMES SQUARE. THAT'S NUTS.

WELL, IF WE NAP IN ROTATIONS, THEN TWO PEOPLE CAN STAY AWAKE FOR AN HOUR AND WATCH OUR STUFF AND THE OTHER ONE CAN SLEEP. WE'LL DRINK COFFEE.

NO. THAT'S A **TERRIBLE** IDEA.

IT WAS SO HOT YESTERDAY, HOW IS IT SO COLD TODAY?
SIXTY IS NOT THAT BAD. IT MIGHT RAIN LATER, THOUGH.

SO, YOU'RE WORKING AT THE POOL THIS SUMMER? THE MANAGERS THERE WERE ON THE SWIM TEAM WITH ME. THEY'RE HILARIOUS—YOU'RE GONNA LOVE THEM.
YEAH, EVERYONE ON STAFF THERE IS HOT.
I'M REALLY EXCITED. THEY OPEN WHEN THE PUBLIC SCHOOLS LET OUT, SO I MIGHT DO A LITTLE LANDSCAPING BEFORE THEN OR ELSE I'M GOING TO GET BORED TO DEATH. I MEAN, MY PARENTS GO TO BED AT 9:30. I'M ALREADY BORED, AND I'VE ONLY BEEN HOME FOR A WEEK.
SNORE
I LOVE IT HERE. IT'S SO LOUD. THERE'S SO MUCH GOING ON. I CAN'T BELIEVE WE SURVIVED ALL THE SUBURBAN SILENCE.
MINNEAPOLIS ISN'T EVEN THAT BIG OF A CITY, AND HOME FEELS LIKE A GHOST TOWN IN COMPARISON. YOU CAN HEAR EVERY FLOORBOARD IN MY PARENTS' HOUSE.
WHEN DID I START SAYING "MY PARENTS' HOUSE"?

WELL, MY HOUSE WON'T BE SILENT UNTIL LENA GRADUATES FROM HIGH SCHOOL.
BUT THEN THERE'S STILL THE DOGS.

I LOVE YOUR HOUSE.
ME TOO.

SCREEEETCH!
I WONDER WHEN WE'LL ALL BE TOGETHER LIKE THIS AGAIN.
THE HOLIDAYS, PROBABLY.
GO HOME, YUPPIES!
HONK HONK
HONK
HONK

I'LL STILL BE IN AUSTRALIA. I DON'T KNOW WHEN I'M COMING BACK.
BUT WE'LL BE TOGETHER AGAIN SOMETIME SOON, RIGHT?

YEAH.
PROBABLY.
FLICK
FLICK

CAN I TAKE THIS SWEATER HOME WITH ME?
SURE, I'LL GET IT AT CHRISTMAS.
THUD
FLOP

KNOCK
KNOCK

HEY, YOU, HOW WAS THE TRIP?

FUN.

FUN? THAT'S ALL I GET? ALL THOSE ENGLISH CLASSES AND YOU CAN ONLY MUSTER ONE WORD?

I DIDN'T GET ANY SLEEP ALL WEEKEND. I THINK I'M GETTING SICK.

AH.
DO YOU WANT TO GO FLOAT? MY BACK IS KILLING ME.
SCRATCH
SCRATCH

WHEN DOES LIFE STOP BEING LIKE THIS?

LIKE WHAT? TAKING SPONTANEOUS FREE TRIPS WITH YOUR FRIENDS? PRETTY SOON.
NO, LIKE...YOUR FRIENDS MOVING AWAY AND STUFF.

MMM.
ON AND OFF FOREVER.

MMM.

PEOPLE ARE GOING TO COME IN AND OUT OF YOUR LIFE. I MEAN, SOMETIMES I DON'T HEAR FROM FRIENDS FOR YEARS, BUT THAT DOESN'T MEAN WE DON'T STILL LOVE EACH OTHER. PEOPLE GET BUSY.

BUT AREN'T YOU SAD WHEN THEY LEAVE? IT'S SO SAD.

WELL, YEAH, I'LL ADMIT IT'S SAD WHEN DEBBAH LEAVES EVERY YEAR. WE BOTH GET A LITTLE TEARY. BUT SHE COMES BACK, I GO VISIT.
BBBBBB

DID YOU KNOW I USED TO CRY EVERY SINGLE TIME WE LEFT GRANDMA AND GRANDPA'S HOUSE? WHEN THEY'D STAND ON THE DRIVEWAY AND WAVE AT THE CAR, I ALWAYS CRIED.
I DIDN'T KNOW THAT.

THAT'S HOW I FEEL WITH EVERYTHING. EVERYONE ELSE SEEMS LIKE THEY CAN HANDLE CHANGE SO WELL. THEY CAN MAKE REALLY BIG CHANGES AND BE FINE. FOR ME, ALL OF IT IS JUST SO MUCH. I'M ALWAYS THE ONE CRYING IN THE CAR.

WHEN YOU GET OLDER, THINGS WON'T FEEL AS BAD AS THEY DO WHEN YOU'RE 18. THE HIGHS AREN'T SO HIGH, AND THE LOWS AREN'T SO LOW. DON'T WORRY SO MUCH ABOUT YOUR FRIENDS.

I WORRY ABOUT EVERYTHING. IT'S NOT JUST FRIENDS. IT'S EVERYTHING.

I JUST FEEL LIKE I FAILED THIS YEAR. I DISAPPOINTED EVERYONE. I OVERDID EVERYTHING IN HIGH SCHOOL AND THEN GOT TO COLLEGE AND I'M...NOBODY. I DIDN'T JOIN CLUBS, I TRIED TOO HARD, AND THEN I DIDN'T TRY ENOUGH, AND I DID ALL THIS STUFF TO BE BETTER, BUT I'M STILL...

YOU REMIND ME A LOT OF GRANDMA.
OUR FAMILY IS A LITTLE INTENSE.
BUT THAT ALSO GIVES US DRIVE. YOU JUST CAN'T LET IT RUIN YOUR LIFE. YOU HAVE TO TAKE THE GOOD WITH THE BAD.

EVERYBODY'S GOT SOMETHING THAT MAKES IT HARD FOR THEM TO MOVE FORWARD. YOU KNOW WHAT I MEAN?

I GET IT.

YOU'VE ALWAYS BEEN A TOUGHIE. EVERYTHING IS GOING TO WORK OUT.
OK.

SO, ARE YOU UP FOR A LITTLE BAD RAGAZ?

my sustainable life :)
HOW'S BIG TOE?
FINE. KINDA TIRED.
WHAT ARE YOU LOOKIN' AT?
NOTHING. A VIDEO.
I BROUGHT YOU AN ORANGE.
THANKS.

IT'S NICE TO HAVE YOU HOME. I'M PROUD OF YOU.
DID MOM TELL YOU TO SAY THAT?
PAT
PAT

NOOOO.

NO.
IT'S JUST NICE TO HAVE YOU HOME.

HOP

GOT ANY *JEOPARDY!* TAPED?

YOU SHOULD KNOW THIS ONE.
I DON'T.

WHAT IS MADAME BOVARY?
YOU HAVEN'T READ MADAME BOVARY? WHAT ARE THEY TEACHING THESE DAYS?
WELL, DAD, I HAVEN'T READ EVERY BOOK.

ALL RIGHT, SOMEONE SCOOT OVER.

WHO IS HERODOTUS?
SCOOT
SCOOT
I KNEW THAT ONE.

SARAH'S 19TH BIRTHDAY.
I KNOW IT'S NOT A BIG SURPRISE, BUT I SAW THIS AND IT MADE ME THINK OF YOU.
BOUND SKETCHBOOK
IT'S BEAUTIFUL!
THANKS, MOM.

I GUESS WE ALL HAD THE SAME IDEA.

THIS IS HONESTLY A BEST-CASE SCENARIO FOR ME.

PING!
PING!

1:45pm
Hapee Burfdae :))) luv uuu
Happy Bday biiiittchhhh! Miss ya ;)
hbd
HBD Srah! Can't wait to see you on campus this fall! :)

SHOOT, I BETTER LEAVE FOR MY SHIFT. TELL LINDA THANKS FOR THE LUNCH—IT WAS REALLY NICE!

WILL DO. I'LL SEE YOU TOMORROW!
PACKING AT TWO?

YES! AND
HAPPY BIRTHDAY!

BUMP

THERE SHE IS. DO YOU WANT TO JOIN ME AND THE DOGGO FOR A WALK?
MAYBE LATER. I'M GETTING PICKED UP IN A FEW MINUTES.

HUEY SAYS YOU'RE MISSING OUT.
OH, HE TOLD YOU THAT?

SORRY, HUEY.
SMOOCH

YOU KNOW WHAT I JUST REALIZED?

IT'S YOUR LAST YEAR BEING A TEENAGER!

PING!

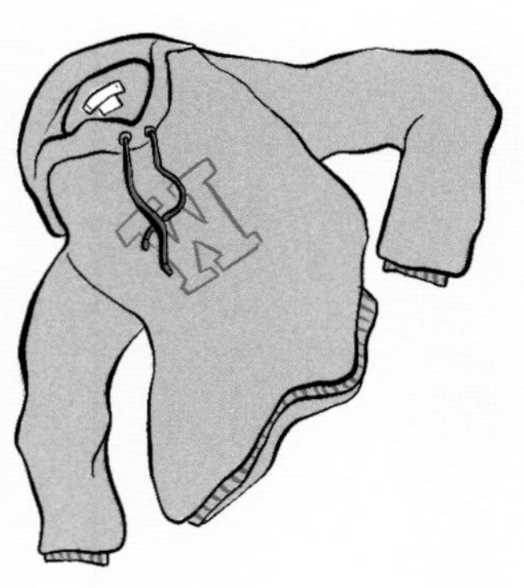

EPILOGUE

Freshman Year doesn't build to a tidy conclusion. The arc of this story deviates from a classic sequence of conflict, climax, and resolution. There are blurry boundaries of emotional beginnings and endings, unanswered questions, and loose ends.

This same nebulous feeling of uncertainty lives in my memories of college. In some ways, creating a clear narrative of "what happened and why" seems artificial. This time in my life was defined by a looseness, a sense of ebbing and flowing and unsatisfying outcomes.

College was a string of disparate moments with contrasting tones. A night of carefree fun could mutate into a spiral of existential dread. A day of contemplating literary theory could end in watching a Nickelodeon movie. Over time, my solid sense of self melted into something amorphous. Understanding this seemed impossible, and when asked, "How was your freshman year?" I often felt like there was no good answer.

I had no monumental romance, no huge academic achievement. Nothing permanently tragic or fantastical occurred. The story that evolved was a collection of small growths and failures, staggered in no clear order.

So it stands to reason that this book begins with an ending and ends with a beginning. Sarah leaves these pages going into summer with more questions than answers, with hope and with anxiety, with friendships ahead and beside and behind. Facing head-on whatever lies beyond the horizon: the rest of life.

AUTHOR'S NOTE

This story was assembled by poring over journals, sketchbooks, posts, photos, homework assignments, and conversations from my freshman year at college. Whittling down one year into a single narrative is complicated, especially if that period was…well, all over the place. That's why this story is both truth and fiction.

After organizing my material came the business of transforming it all into a coherent read. It turns out memories alone are not very compelling. The fictional elements of this book serve to remedy that issue and a few others. Some names have been changed and locations obscured to protect the privacy of my friends and family. Time lines had to be altered, certain events left out or combined. I created composite characters to avoid an overwhelmingly large cast: Liz was inspired by about seven different people, and I had crushes on many, many people like Robby. Unfortunately, I could not write about everyone.

My goal had always been clear: to share how that year felt, the good and the bad. I had gone through some of my highest highs and some of my lowest lows, and came out of the experience feeling uncertain and embarrassed. I felt I had failed to leave my emotional baggage at home, to transform into something different from the secretly anxious, depressive person I had been in high school. Despite my attempts at growth, I had not lived up to my own expectations and the expectations I assumed other people had for me.

After my freshman year, I listened to stories from friends and family that reflected my experiences back to me. People who appeared to have had a great time revealed that they had struggled in very similar ways: managing their mental health, feeling the pain of relationships changing or ending, coping with new shades of loneliness, trying out scary and exciting identities. These milestones had unfolded for all of us, mixed in with the daily rhythm of life.

I hope that you feel reflected in these pages, too. And that you have a bit of a laugh along the way.

WORDS OF THANKS

Thank you to Lori Nowicki and Claire Morance at Painted Words for their belief in my idea back when it was just a seedling. Many thanks to my editor, Jessica Anderson, whose sharp wit and enthusiasm made each step of the process much less scary, and whose emails always put a smile on my face. This book was beautifully assembled by the incredible team at Christy Ottaviano Books / Little, Brown Books for Young Readers, including Jake Regier, Ann Dwyer, and Megan McLaughlin, whose close attention and care have never gone unnoticed. Thank you for making it all happen.

A very special thank-you to the friends and family who graciously allowed me to write about our relationships. Clea, David, Jaysen, Maddy, and Yù Yù: thank you, thank you, thank you. You have all been exceedingly cool about everything, and I promise not to do it again. Oliver, I am eternally grateful for your silliness, kindness, patience, love, and gentle reminders to go outside.

Thank you most of all to my parents for your abundance of love and support—I owe it all to you. I could never thank you enough for everything. Thank you, I love you.

Photo by Sarah Mai

SARAH MAI

is an illustrator and writer based in Minneapolis, Minnesota. She has a degree in English literature from the University of Minnesota, Twin Cities, where she developed a passion for graphic novels. She is the illustrator of *The Cool Code and The Cool Code 2.0: The Switch Glitch. Freshman Year* marks her author-illustrator debut.